A Home Subscription! It's the easiest and most convenient way to get every one of the exciting Coventry Romance Novels! . . . And you get 4 of them FREE!

You pay nothing extra for this convenience: there are no additional charges. . .you don't even pay for postage! Fill out and send us the handy coupon now, and we'll send you 4 exciting Coventry Romance novels absolutely FREE!

SEND NO MONEY, GET THESE
FOUR BOOKS
FREE!

- -

C0182

**MAIL THIS COUPON TODAY TO:
COVENTRY HOME
SUBSCRIPTION SERVICE
6 COMMERCIAL STREET
HICKSVILLE, NEW YORK 11801**

YES, please start a Coventry Romance Home Subscription in my name, and send me FREE and without obligation to buy, my 4 Coventry Romances. If you do not hear from me after I have examined my 4 FREE books, please send me the 6 new Coventry Romances each month as soon as they come off the presses. I understand that I will be billed only $9.00 for all 6 books. There are no shipping and handling nor any other hidden charges. There is no minimum number of monthly purchases that I have to make. In fact, I can cancel my subscription at any time. The first 4 FREE books are mine to keep as a gift, even if I do not buy any additional books.

For added convenience, your monthly subscription may be charged automatically to your credit card.

☐ Master Charge
42101

☐ Visa
42101

Credit Card #_____

Expiration Date_____

Name_____
(Please Print)
Address_____

City _____ State _____ Zip _____

Signature_____

☐ Bill Me Direct Each Month **40105**
Publisher reserves the right to substitute alternate FREE books. Sales tax collected where required by law. Offer valid for new members only. Allow 3-4 weeks for delivery. Prices subject to change without notice.

THE GHOST
and
LADY ALICE

by

Marion Chesney

FAWCETT COVENTRY • NEW YORK

THE GHOST AND LADY ALICE

Published by Fawcett Coventry Books, a unit of CBS
Publications, the Consumer Publishing Division of CBS Inc.

Copyright © 1981 by Marion Chesney

ISBN: 0-449-50237-6

Printed in the United States of America

First Fawcett Coventry printing: January 1982

10   9   8   7   6   5   4   3   2   1

For Charlie,
My son,
With love.

THE GHOST
and
LADY ALICE

ONE

Wadham Hall stood high among the Sussex downs, a magnificent example of Elizabethan architecture. Its structure was a rectangular block with six towers. It was surrounded by walled courtyards and gardens, turrets and gatehouses. Since it had been built in an age when glass was a status symbol, it was more glass than brick, its mullioned windows blazing in the sun.

All this magnificence was the property of the Tenth Duke of Haversham. He entertained in a lavish style and his house parties were legendary. His guests considered themselves honored to be invited. The Hall was beautifully run with every luxury and comfort, as an army of servants flitted silently to and fro, catering unobtrusively to every need.

The upper servants did not consider their life very hard although they worked long hours. At least they were housed and fed.

But the lower order of servants lived in a state which was little more than slavery. Their wages were practically nonexistent, there was no escape for them for there was little other work to be had in the surrounding countryside, their living quarters were disgraceful, and they cringed under the all-powerful tyranny of the Groom of the Chambers, Mr. Bessant.

But there is a lot to be said for having never known anything better, and certainly that was so in the case of Alice Lovesey, the little scullery maid.

At least, not that she could remember.

She could certainly remember the hard, calloused feel of the hand that had pulled her toward the servants' wing of Wadham Hall, but could remember nothing more about the person who had brought her there. She remembered it had been a cold evening, probably autumn, and that the many windows of the Hall had burned in the setting sun like a sheet of flame, and she had cried aloud with terror and had been cuffed into silence.

Alice guessed she must have been about twelve years old at the time. What had been her life before that day was a complete blank. The awesome personage who had conducted her to the Hall had said something about "found wandering." Her name was Alice

Lovesey because they had found that information on a label pinned to her ragged clothes. Her feet had been cut and bleeding as if she had been walking for a long time. No one knew of a Lovesey family anywhere in the neighborhood. The girl was not of gentle birth for she had a country burr. And so that was that. She was hired as scullery maid and tied body and soul to the lower regions of Wadham Hall. Alice found one day that she could read and write and that seemed to her a marvelous thing, but she did not mention this fact to the other servants since she had discovered that to do anything that brought one to the notice of the others, usually resulted in blows and torments and extra work.

For it is a sad fact that a bad master hires bad servants. The Duke was callous, cruel, thoughtless and arrogant, and so the upper servants were hired in his image and brutalized the lower servants in *their* image, and so all the unhappiness went down the chain of command and fell on the shoulders of the very bottom layer who had no one to be nasty to but each other.

Despite the drudgery, Alice had grown and survived and had been at the Hall for seven long years. It is possible that she might have been quite a beauty if she ever had the leisure to clean herself but, as it was, she appeared to the others as a dirty, insignificant creature who never spoke.

One day when the Duke and Duchess of

Haversham had an even larger house party than usual, tempers in the kitchen were running high. The guests had arrived two weeks ago and seemed destined to stay forever. For two weeks the servants had been run ragged, carrying slops, carrying hot water, carrying meals for what seemed like twenty-four hours a day since some of the guests stayed up all night, while the others rose early to hunt or shoot.

Then horror of horrors! One of the guests had found a cobweb in his chamber pot and had complained of it to the Duke. The Duke had sent for the Groom of the Chambers and had given him a tongue-lashing. The Groom of the Chambers had in turn insulted the butler, who had berated the housekeeper, who had screamed at the head footman, who had cursed the other footmen, and so on, until the Cook had given Alice a public whipping in the middle of the kitchen, for someone had to take the blame.

Just when the beating was over, it was announced the guests would depart at the end of the week. Anger subsided, tempers cooled and Alice crawled off to her pots and pans, white-faced and trembling, feeling so hurt in body and soul that she wondered if she would live and, at the same time, praying she might die.

Further good news was announced. His Grace and his guests were driving out that evening to visit a neighbor and would not be expected back until late the next day. The servants would be able to go early to bed.

Alice bent over her work, dimly hearing the joyful cries in the kitchen and hating every single servant in the Hall, and hating the Duke with all her little heart. It was new for Alice to hate. So far she had accepted the drudgery of her life as part of her place in the divine plan. But that beating had been the final straw. She hated the Duke because he was completely indifferent to the plight of any lesser being in the social order. She hated the Groom of the Chambers—she hated them all.

For the first time in her life, she wanted to escape. For the first time in her life, she thought rebelliously that she was meant for better than this.

But as usual she said nothing, working steadily, working late until the "goodnights" sounded from the kitchen, working over the pots by the light of one smelly tallow candle until she heard all the voices die away.

Her bed now waited for her—if you could call it a bed. It was nothing more than an evil-smelling straw pallet which was kept rolled up in a corner of the scullery. She was expected to sleep neatly and quietly in the corner of the scullery and to awaken, as if by magic, at four in the morning no matter how tired she was.

Alice had never seen any other part of the house but the kitchen. She had never been further away from the house than to the pump in the backyard. She was not even allowed to go to church with the other servants because she was expected to stay behind with two other drudges and prepare their Sunday dinner.

She was so tired and sore and angry that she felt quite light-headed, and perhaps that is what gave her the courage to creep across the blackness of the kitchen and slowly mount the stairs to the upper region.

Now the Hall was said to be haunted by the ghost of the Eighth Duke who had broken his neck in a hunting accident around the year 1751. The next Duke, the Ninth, had been as much a tyrant as the present one and he had died of an apoplexy in 1789 and nothing in his life had become him like the leaving it. He had no direct heir and so the dukedom and the title and all, had gone to a distant relative, now the present Duke, who was supposed to bear a marked likeness to the Eighth, being handsome in a haughty and arrogant way.

But there, evidently, the resemblance ceased. For the Eighth Duke had been a wastrel and rakehell, but had had a reputation for having been kind and generous to his servants. He had also been a tremendous ladies' man. The present Duke was married to a chilly, high-nosed wife who suited him very well. He was nasty to his servants, but had never seen the inside of a gambling hell or got up to any of the wild antics of his ancestor.

There had been stories in the kitchen that the Eighth Duke still walked the empty corridors of the Hall at night, but Alice somehow was not afraid of meeting a ghost. The horrors of the present world were terrifying enough without starting to be frightened of some poor spirit who probably did not exist anyway.

She timidly pushed open the door of the great hall and stood looking about her in awe. Mellow gold stone seemed to stretch for miles in front of her, lit by the light of one oil lamp placed on a carved oak chest. Tapestries hung silently against the walls, their figures of huntsmen and hounds seeming almost alive in the dim, golden light. A great, carved flight of stone stairs led up from the great hall to the state rooms on the second floor.

Alice felt no fear. It was as if she had passed beyond that state into a kind of limbo where nothing in the outside world could touch her. Her bare feet making no sound on the stone flags, she moved lightly across the hall and mounted the stairs.

Very gently she pushed open the door of the banqueting hall and slipped inside. The huge room was brightly lit by shafts of moonlight streaming in the windows. The walls were decorated with a moulded and painted plaster frieze showing Diana and the animals of the forest. The figures had many bright

15

painted eyes which seemed to follow the progress of the little scullery maid across the room.

Unlike the other rooms of the Hall, this one had only one portrait. It was hung between the windows. Alice pulled out a great carved chair at the end of the banqueting table and looked down the hall to the portrait.

But the portrait was in the shadow between the two windows. Still, with that feeling of unreality, she lit a branch of candles and carried it over to the portrait, reading the brass plate underneath first.

"Gervase, Eighth Duke of Haversham," she read aloud. She raised the candelabra and looked up at the picture.

He was certainly somewhat like Alice's present master with his high-nosed handsome face. But where the present Duke's face was cold and his eyes pale, this man's eyes held a mocking glint and his mouth was curved in a smile. He was dressed in the clothes of the period in which he had lived, gold brocade coat with lace foaming at his throat and wrists, silk knee breeches and powdered wig. He had his hand on his sword hilt, and behind him, the artist had faithfully painted the magnificence of Wadham Hall.

Suddenly Alice realized what she was doing and where she was. She would be thrashed within an inch of her life if they found her here. The candelabra shook in her hand and she looked from the portrait to it in dawning horror. It was made of solid gold. Perhaps they would accuse her of stealing and she would surely be hanged.

She turned to flee but something made her turn slowly round and look back up at the picture. It was a kind face, she decided.

"Oh, I wish you was here now, sir," said Alice. "I wish to God you was!"

With a little sigh, she turned away from the portrait and walked back toward the banqueting table to replace the candelabra.

Gervase, Eighth Duke of Haversham, was seated in the high-carved chair at the head of the banqueting table. There was an expression of stunned surprise on his handsome face. Alice stood hypnotized, one part of her mind wondering why she felt no fear.

The Duke stretched out an elegant leg encased in a clocked stocking and ending in a diamond-buckled shoe with a high red heel and studied it carefully. Then he tossed back the lace at his wrist and pinched himself with long, delicate white fingers. Then he shrugged and felt in the capacious pocket of his coat, pulled out a snuffbox, looked at it with surprised delight, took a pinch of snuff and sighed with pleasure.

"Stap me vitals," said the Duke in a light, amused voice. "It's I, in the flesh. Back again. Odd's Fish!"

Alice approached timidly. "Are you a ghost?" she said in a croaky voice.

The Duke stared down the banqueting hall

at the ragged girl, holding the branch of candles.

"I suppose I must be. Come hither, child."

Alice moved slowly toward him. She must be dreaming or perhaps the present Duke was playing some mad joke. But as she neared him she saw his eyes were a very dark vivid blue, so this could not be her master. "I'm dreaming," thought Alice, "so there is nothing to be afraid of." And certainly the whole thing seemed unreal. The staring figures on the frieze on the wall, the elegant gentleman in his antique clothes who was watching her with indulgent amusement.

Alice slowly replaced the candelabra on the table and stood next to him. "Who are you?" asked the Duke.

"Scullery maid an please Your Grace." whispered Alice.

"I' faith, but you are extremely dirty and ragged even for a scullery maid."

Alice blushed. "T'ain't my fault," she said and then, rallying, "At least I'm alive."

"Meaning I am not," said the Duke, pinching himself again. "I feel alive. Hold my hand!"

Alice stared down at the white hand with its weight of glittering rings. Perhaps he would pull her down into hell. Her own grubby little hand trembling, she put it into the Duke's. His hand was warm and alive.

"What was it like . . . in the grave?" she whispered.

"I don't know," he said testily. "All I can remember is that cursed horse balking at a stone wall. Up and over I went and hit a great rock. I seem to remember floating out of my body and looking down at myself and thinking I looked cursed ridiculous. That's all."

"You can't be a ghost," said Alice. "Them's transparent and carries chains."

"And moan and walk through walls," he said cheerfully. "I wonder if I can walk through a wall?"

He got to his feet and tittupped on his high heels across the floor—and walked slap bang into the wall and rebounded.

"Dear me," he said rubbing his forehead. "I really am alive. I'll tell you another thing. I'm cursed hungry. Go get me some food."

"I durst not," said Alice. "What if they ketch un and I says I'm fetching for a ghost, they'll send me to the madhouse."

"You're whimpering," said the ghost callously. "Never could abide whimperers. Sit down and don't stand there with your mouth open."

Alice did as she was bid, staring in fascination at his white face and sparkling eyes. He had a small black patch near his mouth and his jewels winked wickedly in the light.

"Did you ... er ... summon me?" he asked.

"I s'pose I did," said Alice. "I mean, Duke's that hard and I had a beating from Cook and folks have said as how you was kind to your servants, so I wished you were back."

"And here I am," he said cheerfully, "in the ghostly flesh so to speak."

"Folks do say," said Alice cautiously, "that you've been seen around afore."

"Do they now?" he said. "Then they're wrong. I think I would have remembered that, you know."

"Are you going to disappear again?" asked Alice.

"I don't know," said the Duke crossly. "What a lot of questions you do ask." He then proceeded to ask some of his own. Who was the present Duke? What was he like? Married? Children? And Alice answered as best she could.

"Don't you want to know about how hard life is for us here?" ventured Alice.

"No, not in the slightest," said the Duke. "There is nothing more boring than a whining, ungrateful servant. Go to sleep. Go off to bed, there's a good girl and leave me to cogitate."

"What's that?"

"Think."

"Oh!" Alice got up reluctantly. He made no move to detain her. She turned at the door and looked rather wistfully back at him. "I did fetch you back," she said softly.

"And that gives you a claim on my time, you grubby fairy? Very well, my kitchen elf. I shall meet you here, every evening at this time."

Alice bobbed a curtsy and slipped as quietly from the room as she had entered. She was suddenly so tired that the stairs seemed to rise up to meet her. Wearily she stumbled back to the kitchen, pulled her mattress from its corner and fell immediately asleep.

The next day Alice was sure it had all been a dream but, dream or not, she could not forget that the phantom of her dream had called her dirty. When all the other servants were at their evening meal, she slipped out to the pump at the back, and, stripping off, scrubbed herself until she felt raw, and soaped her hair, gasping at the bite of cold water as she rinsed it.

When she was finally allowed to escape to her "bed" that night, she lay down with a feeling of anticipation. She expected to be wafted back to that dream banqueting hall where the dream Duke would be waiting for her. But nothing happened. Only exhausted sleep and the waking in the chill dawn to a feeling of loss.

As the day wore on, she saw several of the men gazing at the freshly washed, midnight cloud of black hair which now tumbled down her back and, feeling uneasy, she found a piece of string and tied it up on top of her head in a severe knot. "If only my ghost had really existed," thought Alice, afraid of these new lecherous looks and particularly afraid of the

Groom of the Chambers whose shoe-button eyes had fastened greedily on her budding bosom as she had bent over to lift a pail of water.

But by evening, exciting gossip had filtered down from the upper chambers and it seemed as if the servants' hall was in a fever of excitement. The Duchess had threatened to divorce the Duke. The ladies of the house party had all been throwing the Duke amorous glances, and it had come out in one splendid row that the Duke had managed to pleasure all four of the younger married ones during the watches of the night.

Alice, huddled in the scullery over the pots, suddenly thought she knew who was responsible for this seduction of the married ladies of the party. She felt sure it was the wicked ghost masquerading as the present Duke. But it had been a dream. Hadn't it? She resolved to go to the banqueting hall, just one more time, and *if* he was there, she would give him a piece of her mind.

The butler was in a furious temper because two bottles of his best claret and one bottle of French brandy were found to be missing. Also, a fine raised pie had been stolen from the larder. One accused the other and eventually the blame fell on the small knife boy who was sorely beaten. Since he had laughed maliciously when Alice had received *her* beating, she found it hard to have any sympathy for him.

The house party was due to leave in the morning to make the long journey to London, and so the servants were being allowed to go to bed early. Alice was just finishing her work when a shadow fell across the pots. She turned around and found herself staring up at the cadaverous face of the Groom of the Chambers.

He moistened his lips and stared down at her and his hand slid around her waist.

"Alice! Alice! Where is that good-for-nothing!" cried the angry voice of the Cook, and Alice, with a sob of relief, made her escape.

She could hardly wait for the servants to go to bed, sitting hiding in the shadows so that no one would notice her. At last they were all abed and the great house was quiet.

Alice slipped quietly upstairs, through the great hall and up the stone stairs. Sending up a little prayer, she pushed open the door of the banqueting hall.

Empty.

She gave a disappointed sob and sat down at the table, tired and frightened. A ghost might be a poor sort of friend, but she had felt somehow that they *could* be friends, as if the grave had removed the vast social gulf which lay between them. She arose and walked slowly and miserably through the patches of moonlight to the portrait which hung between the windows.

"Please come back," she urged, staring upward. "Don't let it be a dream!"

"Odd's Fish! Can't you leave me alone?" said a cross voice directly behind her.

Feeling a surge of gladness, she turned around. "Oh, sir! You're back," she cried and then looked at him, wondering for one awful moment whether it was the present Duke. For the ghost was dressed in a magnificent frogged dressing gown and morocco slippers. He was without his wig and his short cropped hair looked silver in the moonlight.

"That voice of yours," he went on, "seems to be able to positively shout in my head. There I was bedrooming in the guise of my descendant. There were the luscious charms of Lady Helen spread out under me. And then you come in and, damme, I have to come here. You've got to stop it, you know."

"*I've* got to stop it!" cried Alice. "What about your philandering?"

"That is my affair—or affairs—my prudish wench. Well, since you are here and I am here, I may as well hear your whinings. Who has been beating you today?"

"No one."

"Well, there you are! Now if I can just . . . er . . . take up where I left off . . ."

Alice sank to her knees and clutched at a fold of his dressing gown. "Oh, please ghost," she cried. "Help me escape from here."

"Help you . . . My dear child, simply open the door and walk out, damme."

"I can't. I have no money. Nowhere to go."

He frowned down at her and then stretched down his hand and pulled her to her feet. He led her to the table and lit the candles and sat down next to her.

"My late wife—may *she* never materialize—went mad before her death and buried her jewels."

"Did you drive her mad?" asked Alice.

"Don't be impudent. No. She drove herself mad. Opium, brandy and mercury in that order. Where was I? Ah, yes, the jewels. Well, she died before me. I knew where she had hidden the jewels, of course. Poor Agnes could never keep anything secret. I left them where they were for it amused me to see the efforts of my relatives trying to find them. I shall show you where they are. You dig them up, take them to a pawnbroker and you'll have money enough for a Duchess."

"Who will accept jewels from me?" cried Alice. "I am a dirty, common scullery maid."

"Yes," said the Duke heartlessly. "And spineless too. I make a very generous suggestion and all you can do is . . ."

"Couldn't you pawn them for me?" said Alice, her eyes shining with hope as she clutched his sleeve. He fastidiously removed her fingers from his arm. "My dear child," he drawled. "I find that I only exist in the hours of darkness. I do not know yet whether I can exist outside Wadham. I am bored and tired of your whinings and whimperings. Besides, I was enjoying myself immensely before you arrived on the scene."

"You are heartless," sobbed Alice.

"Of course, I'm dead," said the Duke reasonably. "Ghosts do not have hearts. I don't know what they do have. But there it is."

He rose from the table and strolled from the room, whistling a jaunty air.

Alice sat for a long time where he had left her. He was a heartless philanderer. She thought of Lady Helen, a voluptuous brunette. It was easy to attract men when one had all the money in the world, and surrounded by servants who had nothing else to do but to dress your hair and sew your clothes and fetch your paint and powder. When one was rich, one could flirt with the men one wanted to flirt with, thought Alice sadly. "But for me, that really is a fate worse than death. If I get with child, then I will be pushed out of doors."

The next day, she resolved not to see the ghost again. The house guests departed and the servants reported that the Duchess was still berating the Duke and the Duke was still pleading his innocence.

Alice scuttled quietly about the kitchen, trying to hide when Mr. Bessant, the Groom of the Chambers, made his stately entrance. But somehow, his dark, little eyes always seemed to be fastened on her in a greedy way.

At last it was night and time for bed. Thanking God for the departure of the guests, the servants took up their bed candles and made their way to their various quarters.

Alice lay down on her pallet and stared up into the blackness of the scullery. She was fully dressed because she had never known the luxury of undressing for bed.

Then all at once she knew she had to try to see the ghost again.

Quietly she rose to her feet and as silently as a shadow, made her way back up to the banqueting hall. She paused on the stairs thinking she had heard a step behind her but, when she turned around, the hall was deserted.

She scuttled on up the stairs only to find the banqueting hall empty. She knew she could not call him. She had not the courage. And he would be angry with her.

Then she heard the door opening and swung around, a smile of welcome on her face. Mr. Bessant, the Groom of the Chambers, made his majestic way into the room and Alice slowly got to her feet, staring at him in fear and horror.

"Well, well," said Mr. Bessant, breathing in an urgent, raspy way. "Our little kitchen wench is trespassing and our little Alice will be whipped within an inch of her life and turned out of doors."

"I haven't done nothing wrong," pleaded Alice.

"Oh, but you have." There was a silver cup lying on the table. Mr. Bessant slowly picked it up and put it in his pocket. "I found you stealing this and took it from you. You'll hang."

"Oh God," said Alice. "Oh, sir, it's a lie."

"Of course it is," he grinned. "But who will believe you? But if you are a sensible girl and do as I tell you, we'll say no more about it."

He suddenly reached out and hooked his finger in the ragged bodice of her dress and pulled her up against him. "Now," he said harshly, fumbling with his other hand at the flap of his trousers.

"Oh, ghost!" cried Alice in her mind. "Please come. Help me!"

She wrenched and struggled and Mr. Bessant drew back and struck her on the mouth with one hand and clubbed her over the side of the head with the other. The blow made her feel sick and faint and, as she reeled trying to regain her balance, he caught her in his arms.

"What the devil is going on here? Zooks! A rape!"

Alice gave a gasp of relief and Mr. Bessant abruptly released her and stared at the vision facing him, his eyes popping. The Duke was wearing his gold coat and his powdered wig and all his jewels. He slowly drew out his sword by its jeweled handle and pressed the point of it to the shaking Groom of the Chambers' throat.

"Unhand the wench and get thee gone or I

will split thy gizzard, thou foul lump of carrion," said the Duke in measured tones.

"Avaunt thee Satan!" cried Mr. Bessant, making the sign of the cross. Now, that was supposed to work when faced with the supernatural, but this ghost had obviously not read the right books and the sword point never wavered.

Mr. Bessant backed toward the door, white and trembling. "You'll burn for this piece of devilry, Alice Lovesey. You'll burn," he whispered and then he ran from the room.

"Now why didn't he think I was his master?" said the ghost peevishly. "I am uncommonly like the present Duke, think you?"

"No," said Alice bitterly. "The present Duke would not have rescued me. And your clothes! You are wearing the same clothes as in your portrait. They will kill me."

There came a great clamor and uproar from below stairs. "Yes," said the Duke thoughtfully. "I think they will. How tedious. Let us go. I shall hide you."

Alice put her hand in his and he led the way out of the banqueting hall at a leisurely pace. Alice cringed against him as a party of servants appeared at the bottom of the grand staircase, brandishing knives and clubs and torches. The Duke looked down at them dispassionately. Then he stretched out his arms.

"Booo!" he said.

The servants screamed in fear and scattered. Until that moment not one of them had believed Bessant's story about a ghost, believing instead that there was some masquerader loose in the Hall.

"It's the wicked Duke come back from the grave!" cried one, and the Duke let out a great horrible laugh which rang round and round the walls.

"That was really rather good," he said in a pleased way, listening to the echoes. "I was quite good at amateur theatricals, you know."

Alice found that her teeth were beginning to chatter. She was all of a sudden filled with superstitious terror of the Duke and at the same time, she knew she had to follow where he led.

He led her through a maze of corridors, then up to the fourth floor and along another series of passages until he finally opened the door of a small empty room. He crossed to the fireplace and pressed something under the mantel. A section of the wall swung open revealing a dark passage.

"Don't be frightened," he said, "It's not witchcraft. I had to hide my mistresses somewhere in the old days. Ah, memories, memories!"

He lit a candle and led the way, Alice creeping after him, trembling with shock.

The passage did not lead straight down to hell as she had feared, but to a pleasant, paneled bedroom with a large four-poster bed.

"Wonder of wonders," said the ghost, jerking back the bedclothes, "It's dusty but not damp. Go to bed, my girl, while I try to light a fire. You're shaking like a jelly."

As Alice began to climb into bed, he said, "Stop! You are surely not going to bed in those dirty clothes. I see you have cleaned yourself somewhat, but those rags are filthy and very probably are full of livestock."

"I allus sleep in my clothes," said Alice weakly.

"Wait there. I shall find you something. I can float did you know? Very quickly. It is quite exhilarating."

He disappeared from the room and Alice waited, shivering and numb. He returned very quickly, carrying a frothy confection of lace and satin over his arm.

"I borrowed this. Put it on," he said, tossing it to her.

"It's still warm," said Alice, "and perfumed."

"Oh, I had great fun collecting it. Do put it on and stop fussing. Ah, here we have wood and a tinderbox. We shall be as cozy as can be." He bent over the fire and Alice crept around the far side of the bed and pulled the hangings closed to act as a screen. The nightgown fell like a whisper around her poor, emaciated body. She pulled at the string that held her hair and let it tumble down about her shoulders.

She shyly walked around and stood next to the Duke who was warming his hands at a crackling blaze.

He looked up at her in surprise and then stood up and put his hands on her shoulders, looking down at her with a wicked smile on his face.

"Why, Odd's Fish, but you are quite beautiful in an undernourished way," he murmured, his hands sliding down over her shoulders.

Then he stiffened as he felt the weals on her back through the thin material of her nightgown. "Zooks!" he muttered. "What cruelty has come to my home.

"Get into bed, child. We shall talk tomorrow night. You must sleep all day for I shall not be able to be seen until dark."

"Where are you going?" whispered Alice.

"To haunt," he said blithely. "To create the fear of hell in the servants' hall. A-haunting we will go!"

Alice crept under the covers. She would never sleep again. For what was to become of her? And then it seemed as if she plunged over a high cliff and headlong down and into the deepest sleep she had ever known.

TWO

There's a lot to be said for toad-eating. See how it can exorcise even the lively ghost of Wadham Hall.

The present Duke, being apprised of the reason for all the rumpus, called all the servants together. In blistering tones, with icy hauteur, he told them in no uncertain terms what he thought of the manifestation of the night before. It was his considered opinion that his staff had been raiding the cellars. His Duchess was no less frosty. Her pale eyes raked the shuffling hangdog servants with contempt. The Groom of the Chambers was given a Severe Warning. Ghosts did not exist except at the bottom of a brandy bottle, when like the proverbial genie, they had been known to emerge along with green snakes and horned devils and the like.

The staff were severely ordered back to their posts with the grim warning that a public whipping and instant dismissal—no matter how high the rank of the servant—would result, should any of them again alarm the ordered calm of the Hall with childish and drunken tales of . . . pah! . . . ghosts.

The staff shuffled out. Mr. Bessant promptly decided that some accomplice of that wretched scullery maid had been playing a trick on him, probably one of the family's by-blows which peopled the countryside. He accordingly took out his humiliation and spite on the next in line, and so it went right down the scale until, if the ghostly Duke had appeared at that moment among them, they would simply have ignored his existence.

Alice awoke to the sound of rain slashing across the window-panes of the room. She had slept late and was very hungry. Had Alice had a less arduous life, she would have been consumed with superstitious fear. But she had recently decided that if there was a heaven, then it had forgotten her and, if hell existed, it must be like the kitchens of the Hall and therefore an evil not to be feared since she was already well acquainted with it.

As far as she was concerned, she was warm and rested for, it seemed, the first time in her life. She was used to hunger pangs since often she was not allowed to cease her toil in order to eat. So she settled herself in the great bed to await the return of the ghost neither worrying about the day before, or fearing the day to come.

She did not know in which part of the great house this secret room was hidden. It was at the top, that she knew from looking out of the window.

Alice's first feelings of unease started as dusk fell and the shadows began to lengthen. What if her ghost, her Duke, vanished as mysteriously as he had arrived? She realized she was still wearing the nightgown and hurriedly, but with reluctance, changed back into her rags.

The room grew very black and she could not find the tinderbox he had used the night before to light the fire. She climbed back into bed, wrapping the coverlet about her, and stared into the darkness, waiting and waiting.

"Now, what are we to do with you?" said a voice in her ear and she nearly leaped through the bed canopy in fright.

"Is that you, Your Grace?" she whispered.

"The late one," rejoined that now familiar mocking voice. He lit a branch of candles on the table.

At first Alice almost did not recognize him. He had found a suit of clothes in the current mode, blue swallowtail coat, leather breeches and glossy Hessian boots. His snowy cravat was intricately tied and his close-cropped hair which had looked silver in the moonlight, turned out to be gold.

"What do you think?" he asked, turning slowly around in front of her.

"Very fine," said Alice nervously. He looked so real, she began to wonder if it were not after all some relative of the Duke's playing tricks.

"Thank you," he said sedately. "I'Faith, it is a dreary fashion, I think. I prefer silks and satin and lace. This jacket is so tight, I had a monstrous hard job getting into it. I stole it from the present Duke's wardrobe. Of course, he is so determined to excuse and explain away my existence that he will in all probability not mention it."

"He will accuse one of the servants," said Alice.

"No he will not. For he knows I exist. I talked to him tonight. I told him exactly what I thought of him and he listened to me very carefully and then he said, 'There are no such things as ghosts, therefore I do not believe in you, I do not see you or hear you and so it will continue until you cease to plague me.' Odd's Life! What a cold fish. He has not even the imagination necessary to be frightened!"

"What is to become of me?" said Alice in a dreary voice.

"I don't know," said the ghost crossly. "Stop crouching and whimpering in that bed."

"I'm cold."

"Then I shall light a fire."

"I'm hungry."

"So am I," he replied with surprise, "although I cannot understand why. I shall attend to the fire first, then the food and then your future. I can leave the Hall, by the way. I paid a very pleasant visit to my graveside. The tombstone is a trifle florid, I admit . . ."

"You are a ghost," said Alice, shaken suddenly with superstitious dread.

"Of course I am, you silly chit. Hadn't we already established that? I am not going to breathe brimstone on you or drag you off to the devil if that is what troubles you."

Alice climbed slowly from the bed as he lit the fire. "It don't seem natural," she ventured.

"No," he agreed pleasantly. "But you are better off here with me than slaving in that kitchen. You are hungry, which is why you are whining in that vulgar way of yours more than usual. Faugh! Those clothes of yours are going on the fire as soon as I have a blaze going."

Alice clutched her clothes to her. "Don't touch me!" she cried. "T'ain't decent . . ."

"Oh, I do not have evil designs on you, my kitchen wench. Only on those horrible garments. I shall fetch you something else. Which color of gown I wonder? Blue, I think." And then he was gone.

Alice blinked. She was sure he had not opened the door. She crouched in a chair by the fire and waited.

He returned as suddenly as he had disappeared, bearing a heavy tray in one hand and a pile of clothing in the other. "Put these on," he commanded, throwing the clothes on the bed.

Alice picked them up and cautiously retreated behind the far side of the bed and drew the curtains. The underthings were of fragile India muslin and the gown was of blue silk.

"I hope you do not catch your death of cold," came the ghost's voice from the other side of the bed. "What a marvelous age this is! Never have women worn so little. I do not approve, however. I like more left to the imagination. They do not wear what I would call gowns these days, but things more like shifts."

Alice emerged cautiously in her new clothes. He turned and surveyed her for a long moment. She was very thin but her hair was magnificent and her eyes seemed very wide and dark in her thin face. The blue gown was a trifle large for her and inclined to slip at the shoulders. Alice had never worn such fine, thin material before and felt almost naked.

She nonetheless felt very grand and ladylike for this was surely one of the Duchess's gowns, and was disappointed when the ghost merely stared at her curiously for a few moments and then busied himself uncorking a bottle of wine.

"Do I look like a lady?" she asked timidly.

His very bright blue eyes raked over her. "No," he said after due consideration. "You look like a kitchen maid in one of her mistress's gowns. Now, don't look so miserable. You are quite pretty in a half-starved way. Pull up a chair and sit down. The food is cold—a veal pie and a brace of grouse—but we also have wine and bread and a good fire. Then you have my fascinating company. Come, smile. Girls of your class are not usually favored with such exalted company."

"Oh, yes thay are," flashed Alice, suddenly angry. "A certain type o' women."

"Lightskirts? Ah, yes. Perhaps you will become a famous courtesan."

"A what?"

"Never mind. Drink your wine, close your mouth—it is hanging open in a stupid, peasant way—and eat. We will discuss your future later."

Effectively silenced and humiliated, Alice started to eat, handling the knife and fork very awkwardly since she was used to eating with her fingers.

Alice drank a glass of wine very quickly and then another. Like most French wines which had passed through the hands of a London importer, it was heavily fortified with brandy. At first she felt dizzy but, after making a good meal, she began to feel strangely elated. The Duke ate and drank silently, seemingly immersed in his thoughts. The November gales hurled across the downs, throwing icy rain against the window. The fire hissed and crackled and the wavering light from the candles on the table enclosed them in a small pool of light.

Alice found herself wondering idly how it was that the Duke could take his return to life so calmly.

The Duke had not taken it calmly in the least. After his first exaltation at finding himself alive, he had settled down to some serious thought. Why had he been brought back? To atone for his sins? What if his wife, Agnes, should materialize? He shuddered. He could still hear her steady complaints, see her steady disintegration as she removed herself from the world on an opium cloud, surrounding herself with quacks who told her it was necessary medicine for her imagined ills. What was he supposed to do with this half life? As daylight filtered from the east, he simply ceased to exist. There was no dramatic return to the grave. Just nothing. It was all very strange.

And who was this little kitchen maid who had the power to summon him back? He studied her covertly as she bent her glossy black head over her food. She could, perhaps, be a great beauty given a bit more flesh and a great deal of rest. But apart from that, she was very much a kitchen maid with her slow country speech and her red, calloused hands.

He said in a kinder voice than he had used to her before. "What is thy name, child?"

"Alice. Alice Lovesey."

"Thy parents?"

"I don't know," said Alice. "I was brung here when I was twelve, I do reckon. Person who brung me says as how I was found wandering. There was this here liddle note pinned to my dress with my name."

"Lovesey," he said thoughtfully. "I wonder. I do not know of any family of that name about here."

Flushed with wine and comforted with food, Alice clasped her little hands together and stared at him earnestly. "Oh, p'raps I be the daughter of a high-born lady who's a-looking for me still."

"No. You are not high born," said the ghost flatly. "It is possible however your parents were a respectable country couple. You could change, of course. If, say, I trained you to be a lady and found you an establishment in London, then there is no reason why you should not marry well. Dear Agnes's jewels, correctly sold, should set you up with an excellent *dot*.

"It will be difficult to make a lady of you— but not entirely impossible. I shall find you a wardrobe tomorrow. For that, I must go further afield. I think I should cease my haunting of this establishment until you are settled."

"I don't want you to steal things for me," said Alice in a low voice.

"Then I shall leave money for them, my prude. I shall take the present Duke's money and that will not be stealing for, after all, I am only taking what is my own. We shall contrive. I don't suppose you can read or write."

"Oh, yes, sir," said Alice proudly. "I can do both."

"Really!" His thin eyebrows flew up in surprise. "Forgive me if I do not believe you. Wait!"

To Alice's alarm he went straight through the wall and disappeared.

"A new accomplishment," he murmured, returning as abruptly as he had left with a pile of books, paper, pen and ink.

"Now," he said, flicking over the pages of a book. "I shall give you something to read to me and then I want you to write it. Let me see . . ."

He handed her a calf-bound volume of Sir Thomas Browne's *Religio Medici* and pointed to a paragraph with one long, polished nail.

Alice looked at the print, half afraid that this one talent should have deserted her. But the sense of the words leaped immediately to her brain, and she read clearly.

"Whosoever enjoys not this life, I count him but an apparition, though he wear about him the sensible affections of flesh. In these mortal acceptions, the way to be immortal is to die daily."

"Clever man," murmured the Duke. "Very good, my child. Now write what thou hast read."

Alice had never tried to write, that she could remember, but somewhere in the back of her brain, she knew that she could. She dipped the newly sharpened quill in the inkwell, bent over the paper, closed her eyes for a moment in intense concentration and began to write while the Duke watched her carefully. When she had finished, she handed him the parchment and he studied the neat Roman script in surprise.

"A scholarly hand, i'faith," he said. "Thou hast learning somewhere in thy misty past, Alice."

Alice beamed at him proudly. "Then my parents had learning?"

He nodded. "Someone undoubtedly did. I think we have done enough work for tonight. Before you retire, I shall leave you some copies of *La Belle Assemblée* and tomorrow when I am gone, you may pass the day in studying the fashions of London. I shall leave you enough food for breakfast. Ah, you cannot wear that flimsy gown. I shall find you a morning dress."

Alice clasped her hands tightly together when he had left. She felt she should be frightened. But he was the first sympathetic person she had ever met that she could remember and so, at last, she decided to simply accept his ghostly existence without fretting her brains over the reason for this strange and unearthly manifestation.

He was soon back, another gown over his

43

arm. "Put it on," he ordered rather sharply. "I am not yet accustomed to the nakedness of some of these modern gowns and would prefer you more covered."

Alice retreated again behind the screen of the bed. This ensemble was indeed less revealing and more to Alice's taste. It was a plain cambric morning dress, high at the neck and with a short train and let in round the bottom with two rows of worked trimming. A pelisse of green sarsenet, very fitting, went over it. The pelisse was trimmed with fancy trimming and fastened with a gold brooch, confined round Alice's small waist with a girdle of sarsenet with a gold clasp. There was a pair of walking shoes of brocaded silk to go with it, rather large for Alice's small feet. She felt strange wearing shoes, the first time in her life that she could remember having put any on.

She emerged from the back of the bed, hoping the Duke would see a kitchen maid transformed into a lady, but he only looked at her indifferently and remarked that she "would do."

"I shall leave you to your rest," he said, draining off the last of the wine.

"Don't go," pleaded Alice. She all at once did not want to be left alone, and did not somehow want to think of what he might get up to in the hours of darkness.

"You look very tired," he remarked, hesitating by the door.

"Oh, please, if you stay with me, we could talk and then I could sleep all day and not feel so alone," said Alice.

He hesitated and then suddenly smiled at her in a bewitching way which quite took away her breath. "Very well," he said, sitting down by the fire. "What do you think of my room?"

Alice looked around. It was small and paneled and sparsely furnished. But it was grander than anything she had ever known before. Apart from the bed in the corner, there was the table at which they had eaten with two high-carved chairs beside it. The low fireplace was flanked on either side by two easy chairs and there was a tall wardrobe in one corner and a washstand in the other. A portrait of a lady with masses of fine light hair and a vague expression hung over the fireplace. She was wearing the dress of the last century and had two French greyhounds at her skirts. In the background stretched a romantic Italianate landscape with drooping trees, an obelisk, and an approaching thunderstorm.

"Agnes," he said, following her gaze.

"Your wife," said Alice, quickly averting her eyes from the picture in case she should conjure this ghost back from the dead. "Do you miss her very much?" she added in a low voice.

"You are obtuse," he said severely. "I thought I had made it plain that I do not."

"Then why did you marry her?" asked Alice, made bold by the wine she had drunk.

He glared at her haughtily and then relaxed and seemed to smile at himself. "I was about to stand on my ghostly dignity," he said. "I married her, my curious child, because I was well to go at the time. When I came to my senses, I found her insipid, she who had seemed an ethereal angel the night before. Alas! She was of gentle birth and informed me some three months after our delectable night that she was with child. Since I did not love anyone I entered into a marriage of convenience for the sake of the child.

"There was, of course, no child nor could there be, I gather. It was not that Agnes deliberately tricked me. She was simply a liar. It was hard for her to tell truth from lie since she lived in an opium fog most of the time. I tried to stop her habit but she was extremely cunning and finally I became disaffected. She loved scenes. I abhorred them. She was never happier than when berating me in front of my friends. Ah, me! I enjoyed myself in a very wild way with friends of similar inclinations. I slept most of the day then and roistered at night so there is not much changed now I am come back. What a short night I shall have in the summer! If I am still on this earth."

Alice suddenly thought of London, of becoming a society lady and found that the idea terrified her.

"When I go to London," she said timidly, "will you be with me?"

"Of course not," he said stretching out a booted foot to the dying fire. "I should be very much in the way. Your main motive is to become married, remember?"

"But we are so comfortable here," yawned Alice sleepily.

"It is comfortable compared to what you have known. But it would not always be so. You need the company of young people like yourself. How old are you?"

"Nineteen, I reckon."

"I was thirty-two years of age when I died."

"That's not old," said Alice.

He looked at her oddly and then said gently, "We would not be suited; we would never have been suited, you know."

"Because I'm a servant?"

"No. Not that," he said lightly. "I never . . . er . . . had amorous designs on virgins."

"Oh!" Alice felt hurt and fell into a sulky silence, staring at the red embers.

The red glow faded and receded. She was dreamily conscious of being picked up and carried to bed and felt she should protest. And the next thing she knew, the midday sun was streaming in through the diamond panes of the window. There was bread and cheese on a silver tray on the table and a jug of milk.

There were also several back numbers of

La Belle Assemblée. Then Alice realized she could not remember being put to bed.

She was relieved to find she was still fully dressed even to her shoes. The unaccustomed footwear irked her and she kicked her shoes off.

On the marble washstand were two cans of water and a bar of soap. She wondered uneasily what to do with the slops and after some internal debate, tugged open the window. It led out onto a small ledge behind a high parapet topped with obelisks which perhaps explained why the room had remained hidden.

She climbed out gingerly, feeling the bite of frost on her bare feet, and heaved the contents of the chamber pot over the parapet. From far, far below came an anguished howl and Alice scampered hastily back to the safety of the room and shut the window quickly behind her.

She quickly undressed and washed as much of herself as she could, shivering because the water was cold. A fresh stack of logs had been piled up beside the fireplace, and so she lit a fire and, when it was blazing, she ate her breakfast and then began to leaf through the thick plates of the fashion magazines.

But the gowns seemed so rich, so jeweled with their clasps of topaz, gold and amethyst. Surely it took all the jewels in the world to furnish a wardrobe with gowns such as these! Alice longed for a looking glass so that she could experiment with her hair. It was very long, too long, but it had a natural wave. But then all the ladies in the fashion plates had either curls or bunches of ringlets.

Alice nonetheless diligently read every item in the magazine, including an intriguing advertisement for Pear's Celebrated Soap—

The Ladies will find it a most agreeable appendage to the Toilette, and in using they will be convinced that it will render the arms inimitably white, equal, if not superior, to the most celebrated cosmetic. One trial is sufficient to evince its agreeable and salutory effects. Sold in pots at 3 s.

Soon the shadows began to lengthen as the long winter's night settled down over the countryside. Alice opened the window a little to air the room. A cold breeze moved the bed curtains. It carried that metallic smell of threatening snow.

Alice lit the candles and settled down to wait. Then she noticed that her rags were gone. She wondered idly what the Duke had done with them. He had not put them on the fire because there had been no trace of them among the ashes.

All at once, with a fast beating heart, she heard the chink of glass and china and all at once he was there again, smiling down at her and placing a laden tray on the table.

He had reverted to the dress of his period,

having obviously unearthed some of his old wardrobe. He looked very grand in a blue silk coat with a long white quilted waistcoat edged in silver galloon. He wore his powderèd wig and his handsome face was painted and patched and jewels seemed to blaze all over him.

Alice unconsciously sank into a deep curtsy and he answered with a flourish of his lace handkerchief and a deep bow.

"My Lady Alice," he teased. "You see what respect the clothes of my youth engender? Now we shall dine and I shall tell you my plan. *Hot* food, my child. And cakes to delight your young heart. A fine goose is it not? I simply walked into the kitchen and took it. Your friend the Cook threw her apron over her head and quivered like a blancmange.

"But she durst not cry 'Ghost!' or she will lose her employ. I am not in the least sorry for her. She is a coarse devil of a woman but, 'fore George, she cooks like an angel. Oh, use your fingers. You will send the whole plateful on the floor with your amateurish proddings and pokings."

Alice ate a hearty meal, finishing with several cakes and strawberry tartlets. She again drank a great deal too much strong wine, and between that and the heat from the fire and the magnetic presence of the Duke, she felt as if she were living in some highly colored dream from which she must soon awake and find herself lying on the scullery floor.

"Now," said the ghost, pouring her a bumper of brandy, "A toast. Spirits to the spirit!"

Alice took a sip and choked. He suddenly leaned across the table and took the glass from her.

"Too much for you, my child. I forgot. You are but a babe. See, I have brought lemonade which is what I meant to pour you in the first place. Now—to business!"

Alice sighed a little. She did not want to be reminded that there was a future outside this cozy room.

"French!" he said, producing a small pile of volumes. "You are to become French."

"But I be English," protested Alice.

"Yes. Yes. But how am I to eradicate that country burr of yours in such a short time? Much easier to learn another language. And, after all, it is a good background for you. There are still many titled French émigrés in London selling their jewels to supply them with an income. You, my Alice, shall become Alice, Comtesse de la Valle-Chenevix. Alice is an English name, but there are many French families who once considered it chic to give their offspring English or Irish names. So Comtesse, let us begin."

"I'll never do it, that I won't," sniveled Alice.

"Stop that this instant!" snapped the ghost. "Here is a handkerchief. It is to be used for wiping your nose when you whimper and do not let me catch you wiping your nose on your sleeve again. Faugh!"

"Oh, leave me alone!" wailed Alice, red with shame. "I'll never be a lady."

"Then get back to the kitchens where you belong, you spineless baggage," he said heartlessly. "This is what comes of bestowing my distinguished time and attention on a sniveling . . ."

"Stop!" cried Alice, covering her ears. "I'll do it!"

"That's better," he said looking at her coldly and Alice looked back and suddenly knew she would do anything just so long as he smiled at her again.

She diligently struggled over the primers and because she had slept late, managed to stay up most of the night.

As the days flew past and the north wind piled snow in great drifts up around the Hall, Alice and her ghost worked night after night on her French lessons.

The Duke was amazed at the girl's quick progress. Provided he could get her to speak in English with a French accent, she would soon be ready. He coaxed her in how to walk, how to carry a shawl, how to flirt with a fan, how to make conversation and when to listen. She was taught the value of jewels and laces and how to wear colors best suited to her dark hair and increasingly white skin.

All at once it was Christmas and the Duke

arrived as soon as dark fell with the news that there was to be a great masked ball held in the Hall that very evening.

"And we shall both go," he said sternly, looking down at Alice. "First I must arrange your hair. Pah! I feel like a man-milliner. What days of rest are due to me after I rid myself of you!"

He turned away to heat the curling tongs and therefore did not notice the tearful hurt on Alice's face.

At last he declared himself ready and ordered her to undress to her petticoat until he arranged her toilette, and Alice did so meekly and with a queer little pang at her heart as she knew he would treat her as impersonally as any lady's maid.

"We shall not be announced," he went on, plying the curling tongs and filling the small room with the smell of hot hair. "We shall simply slide through the walls and mingle with the guests. Being a ghost has many advantages."

"You won't go off and leave me," pleaded Alice. "I mean you won't go off with one of them pretty ladies?"

"Don't cling," snapped the ghost, pushing her head roughly forwards and applying the curling tongs to the hair at the back. "Now Agnes clung enough for a squadron of women."

At long last, he pronounced himself satisfied, tipped her face up and gave her a light, playful slap on the cheek.

"Do not look so frenzied, my child," he mocked. "Odd's Fish! What's to be so exercised over? A mere ball! And I shall not leave your side. There! I have made you smile at last. Your gown is on the bed. Wait for me. I must change."

With trembling fingers, Alice slipped on the dress. It was of pale blue gossamer silk worn over a white satin slip. It had a short train at the back and opened up in the front where it was tied with small bows of white satin ribbon. It had long sleeves of pale blue gossamer net, caught down on the outside of the arm with small pearl brooches. The tops of the sleeves and the bosom of the dress were bound with silver edging and trimmed with Valenciennes lace.

The bottom of the skirt and train were edged with a silver edging, and trimmed with the same lace as on the bosom. There was a scarf of pale buff silk ornamented at the end with white silk tassels to go with it. There were also pearl earrings, shoes in pale buff satin and yellow kid gloves.

How Alice longed for a looking glass. She felt very grand and splendid, but she had thought that before and her ghost had not seemed in the slightest impressed.

All at once he was at her side and the pair surveyed each other curiously. Privately Alice thought he had never looked more handsome with his short locks cut in a Brutus crop and his splendid black evening coat and knee breeches. Diamond buckles blazed on his shoes and the lace at his throat and wrists was as fine as cobwebs.

He carried a heavy iron box under one arm which he placed on the table and then stood farther away from her to get a better look at her.

Her once thin face had become heart shaped and her eyes, he noticed were almost violet. The dusky clusters of ringlets accentuated her very white skin which had an almost alabaster pallor from Alice having been confined so long in the room. Her bosom was quite magnificent decided the Duke, putting up his quizzing glass to have a closer look. Alice flushed under his scrutiny and drew the scarf a little more closely about her shoulders.

"You surprise me," was all he would say, but the warmth in his voice made Alice suddenly feel deliriously happy.

He turned from her and opened the strong box and Alice moved closer to him to see what the box contained.

Poor Agnes's jewels blazed up with all the colors of Aladdin's cave.

"Just where she had left them," said the Duke, looking down at them with satisfaction. "Under the outer courtyard wall at the northeast corner. There is thine dowry, child. It pleases thee?"

"It frightens me," whispered Alice.

"Then it is time you became accustomed to

your possessions; I trust we will not have to sell them all.

He looked at her, his blond head tilted to one side. Then he scrabbled in the box and came up with a pearl and diamond necklace which he clasped about her neck.

"Perfect," he said, studying the effect. "Now I have taught you the dances I know. Let us hope they have not changed too much. You will need to dance with other partners, of course, but we will pretend to be a devoted married couple just for this evening."

That somehow was all that was needed to fuel Alice's already blazing happiness.

"Come!" he said, holding out his hand. "It is time to go."

Timidly Alice put her hand on his arm. He led her straight toward the paneled wall.

"I can't go that way," giggled Alice. "I'm not a ghost!"

"If I can take plates of food through walls," he said severely, "then I can most certainly take you."

To Alice, all things were possible that evening and she trustingly allowed him to lead her.

She seemed to melt through the walls as if they were water and then found herself floating gently downward *through* the building.

"Now," he said, coming to a stop in a small anteroom. On the other side of the door, Alice could hear the strains of a waltz.

He drew a black velvet mask from his

pocket and handed her a blue silk one. When they were masked, he took her firmly by the hand. He opened the door.

Lights from hundreds of candles blazed down on them and on the jewels and silks and satins of the guests.

Alice, Comtesse de la Velle-Chenevix had arrived in society.

THREE

It was as well the ghostly Duke did not immediately lead his partner into the dance. For Alice had begun to shake with fear. Her eyes darted from one liveried servant to the other, fearing recognition.

The Duke felt her hand trembling in his and gave it a reassuring squeeze. "We are masked, you know," he said, reading her thoughts. "And were we not, on one would recognize my lady as Alice, the scullery maid. You are a beautiful woman. Come! Look at me and smile. Where are those stars that were in your eyes a bare moment ago?"

He gazed down into her wide eyes, his own warm and reassuring, and Alice felt all her elation and courage flooding back.

"Ah, we have a country dance. *That* we can

do," he said, leading her forward. Unreality took over. Nothing was alive to her but the pressure of this dead man's hand in her own.

The Duke found that he was the one who was nervous as the opening chord struck up. But Alice danced lightly, performing her steps with grace. He was proud of her. Really proud. Through the slits of his mask, he took in the admiring glances cast in Alice's direction. Tomorrow, he would take her to London. And soon he would be free to . . . To do what?

As the dance ended, Alice's hand was quickly claimed for the next by a masked young man. After that, she seemed to move from partner to partner. He contented himself by propping up a pillar and watching her and listening to the easy chatter of her assumed French accent which covered her still frequent mistakes in grammar.

The ballroom at the Hall was much as he remembered it, although all the masked faces, with the exception of the present Duke and Duchess, were strange. He felt suddenly homesick for the old days. He had had little freedom since Agnes's death since he had only survived her by one month. It would have been delightful to have married again, someone young and charming.

He became aware that he had been joined by Alice. "The next dance is a waltz and I do not know how to perform it," she whispered.

"We shall watch," he answered, "and mayhap we shall learn."

After a few moments, he bent his head close to hers and murmured, "It is easy. We shall perform. This new dance pleases me. How it would have shocked my contemporaries."

He swept her into his arms and moved off with her across the floor while lights and colors and music swirled into one heady confection in Alice's bedazzled brain. All she knew was that he had his hand around her waist and now nothing could touch her, nothing could reach her.

When the waltz finished, she stared up at him with eyes like drowned violets. He looked down at her, his own eyes hooded and enigmatic.

"It is time to go, child," he said. "The unmasking is about to begin."

"I say," said Lord Harold Webb, a tall handsome buck to his weedy friend, Harry Russell, "tell me I'm seeing things. That demned pretty little French chit and that tall fellow with the yaller hair just walked through the wall behind those cursed palms."

"You're seeing things," said Harry cheerfully. "Foxed again!"

Back in the hidden room, Alice pirouetted round and round to the sound of the music in her head, watched by the Duke who was unloading the supper which he had stolen from the ball.

"You are ready to fly the coop and test your wings," commented the Duke.

"When must I leave?" asked Alice, suddenly sad.

"Tomorrow."

"So soon?"

"The sooner the better," he said. "You must set up an establishment and find a respectable lady to live with you."

"Why can't you live with me?" Alice burst out.

"It would not answer," he said angrily, uncorking a bottle of champagne with a brisk pop. "Whoever heard of anyone ever living with a ghost?"

"Whoever heard of a ghost?" said Alice gloomily. "I mean not the kind with chains and sheets, but a *living* ghost."

"No one, fortunately," he said amiably. "Perhaps I shall stay quietly here and write my memoirs. Come! Eat your supper. You will not wish to cling to me after you have a few handsome beaux in your train. I am the only person you have to take care of you at the moment, but you will soon forget me."

"Never!" said Alice, her eyes bright with tears.

"What a passionate child it is! Reserve your fervor for your husband. 'Fore George, you are become emotional! It is hunger, nothing more."

"Don't you have *any* feelings," said Alice with a watery smile.

"Oh, yes," he replied. "I did not leave anything at all behind me in the grave, it seems. I have come to the conclusion that I am a mistake of Time. For me, no angels sing or devils torment. Voices do not reach me from above or below. Eat your food, do! I went into the family church last night to pray. I felt afraid all of a sudden of the supernatural which is odd, considering I am supernatural myself. Well, no great light shone on my road to Damascus.

"No great voice cried, 'Repent!' I am here and that is all I know. But I am a practical ghost. I shall simply accept it. Besides, just think of the benefits! We can speed to London through the night air. Think of what we shall save on tolls."

Alice ate her food, listening to him gravely, trying not to be frightened of the day so soon to arrive when he would no longer be with her.

"I have been thinking," he went on, "that it is dark in London at this time of year very early—by five o'clock at the latest. The jewelers' establishments will still be open. I shall masquerade as a French émigré and sell the jewels for you. There! I shall have saved thee at least one ordeal. I shall stay with thee one week masquerading as thine uncle, so do dry thine eyes."

Alice, who had begun to cry, did as she was bid, feeling all at once much happier. He would be with her a further week. She would not think beyond then.

She had a small but rich wardrobe of clothes, procured for her by the Duke, who steadfastly refused to say where he had come by them.

"I have never thanked you properly for all this," said Alice shyly, a small wave of her hand encompassing the room, the wardrobe of clothes, the books and magazines and the food and wine on the table.

The Duke flushed slightly. " 'Tis nothing, my child," he said, his long fingers playing with the stem of his wine glass. "I'Faith, we grow sentimental. I am a selfish ghost. I am looking forward to sampling the modern delights of the ladies of London."

A shadow crossed Alice's expressive little face but either he did not notice, or would not.

"What did you do with my old clothes?" asked Alice after she had managed to control a feeling of hurt which had threatened to make her cry again.

"I put them at the edge of the cliffs along with a suicide note written in an illiterate scrawl. I remember you told me they were not aware of your education. And so ends the life of Alice, scullery maid."

"What if you disappear?" said Alice anxiously. "What would I do?"

"I think I can manifest myself for another week," he said, laughing. "In any case, you have the jewels."

"But you would not be there," said Alice softly.

He put down his glass with an impatient

click and studied her for a while. She cast her eyes down and looked at her plate.

"You are halfway to fancying yourself in love, my sweeting," he said. "It will not do. This is unreality. *I* am unreal. Put me from thy mind, my child. Concentrate your whole being on securing a future for yourself, a home for yourself, a handsome husband and handsome children.

"This unnatural proximity of ours has played tricks with your brain. You are tired and overwrought. You did very well this evening. And I was proud of you. Come! Smile, my Alice. Tomorrow in the clear light of day you will see things differently."

Alice finished her meal as best she could. She could sense that, this evening, he was anxious to be gone. She racked her brains for some topic of conversation to detain him, but could think of none.

At last he stacked the dirty dishes and glasses neatly on the tray as if he had been a servant all his life instead of the master of many.

"Goodnight, Alice," he said formally. "Until tomorrow."

She half raised her hand to try to detain him, but he had already vanished noiselessly through the wall.

"One week," thought Alice. "At least I have one more week."

*   *   *

Alice spent the next day cleaning and tidying the secret room. She felt sad. She felt as if she were leaving the only home she had ever known. Her clothes had gone from the wardrobe, the trunks from the floor. To where he had spirited them she did not know. Surely they could not set about renting a house immediately.

At times poor Alice wondered whether this extra week of his company were a good thing after all. Would it not be better to make a clean break? But surely he could not plan to desert her forever.

Would he not miss her, just a little? And what would he do after he returned? Philander with the houseguests?

She busied herself with her gloomy thoughts and small chores until the shadows lengthened across the floor. He would expect her to be ready. She was wearing a warm quilted gown and an ermine-lined pelisse and swansdown muff lay ready on the bed.

His figure suddenly shimmered for a moment against the dark oak of the paneling and then materialized completely.

"Do your powers never fail you?" asked Alice, trying to joke. "One of these days you might find yourself trapped in the wall."

"It is one of my many tricks," said the Duke proudly. "I discovered I could do it by a simple matter of concentration. Are you ready?"

Alice nodded dumbly and moved to the bed to put on the warm pelisse and tied a smart swansdown-edged bonnet over her curls.

He was dressed in a long, many-caped driving coat and a curly brimmed beaver hat was tilted at a rakish angle on his fair hair.

He waited until she was ready and held out his hand. She looked sadly around the little room for the last time. "At least I have had this," she thought sadly. And then she felt the strength of his long fingers curl about her own.

They melted through the outer wall and out over the grounds of the Hall. Alice gasped and looked down and clutched the Duke's hand tightly.

"You have taken so much in your stride to this date, my sweeting," mocked the ghost. "Do not, I beg you, fail me now. Don't look down."

Alice tried to do as she was bid and soon became a little accustomed to the great rate at which they seemed to be flying over the silent fields. Down below, pinpricks of candlelight from village cottages sparkled and winked in the darkness and, up above them, great stars blazed down in the frosty night.

Villages gave way to larger towns and soon Alice saw the metallic curve of a river sliding below. The Thames, surely.

Then up into the night sky seemed to loom a great black cloud and Alice clutched the ghost's hand tighter and they sped ever nearer toward it.

All at once they were in the midst of a choking, blinding cloud and Alice gasped for breath.

"Stap me vitals!" exclaimed the Duke. "A London fog. We shall descend my dear and try to look for landmarks."

They sailed down, the Duke trying to keep toward the river, glimpses of which occasionally flashed up through the suffocating fog.

At last, "The Monument," he said. "Not long now. Ah, there is St. Paul's. We must float nearly at street level and hope that should anyone see us they will think themselves drunk!"

"Where are we bound?" asked Alice.

"To an hotel, my sweet. The Harland in St. James's. It is as dull and respectable as ever it was. I am thine uncle child. The Comte de Sous-Savaronne, *tu comprends,* hein? Uncle Gervase to you. Our baggage is already ensconced in our rooms. We shall dine, like the respectable couple we are and, then, while you sleep, I shall haunt the empty houses of the fashionable quarter so that we shall be prepared to rent a suitable establishment as soon as we have the money.

"Odd's Fish, 'tis well the nights are long, or I should be hard put to do any business for you. Ah, we are here. At least, I hope we are. This cursed fog does alter things so. We descend now. At least in this murk we shall be able to land at the very door without occasioning comment."

They landed gently on the pavement. By the feeble lights of two parish lamps, Alice could dimly make out the brick facade of the Harland Hotel.

The Duke tucked her arm firmly in his own and together they made their entrance into the hushed foyer of the hotel.

A long looking glass on the wall faced them as they walked in and for one split second Alice did not recognize herself as the modish young lady reflected in the glass.

For some reason, The Duke did not assume a French accent, speaking in his usual impeccable drawling English and leaving the hotel staff to make what they would of it.

He was an imposing and commanding figure, and as he drew off his York tan gloves, his many rings flashed in the candlelight. The manager of the hotel himself was there to conduct them to their suite on the first floor.

It consisted of a pretty sitting room decorated in apple-green and rose. A few bands of fog had managed to penetrate the room, but a large log fire crackled on the hearth with a table for two set in front of it. Two bedrooms led from the sitting room.

"As you see," said the portly little manager, rubbing his hands, "I have Monsieur Le

Comte and milady's bags unpacked and your supper is to be served here as you requested."

Alice nervously opened her mouth to gush forth her thanks but the Duke quelled her with a stern look and nodded pleasantly to the manager, requested his name, learned it was Mr. Perfect, looked mildly amused and firmly bid the manager good evening.

"Now we can be comfortable," said the Duke, rubbing his hands in front of the fire.

"Take off thy mantle, child. Thou lookst frozen to the bone."

Alice shyly removed her pelisse and bonnet, feeling unaccountably nervous at being alone with him in these strange surroundings.

Two footmen entered followed by Mr. Perfect, the manager. They laid several covered dishes on the table and then stood back. The Duke waved them away. "We will serve ourselves," he said. "Do not come back until I send for you."

"There is so much to arrange," ventured Alice when the manager and servants had left.

"We will come about," he said, smiling at her in a way that left her breathless.

It was a silent meal. The Duke, usually talkative, seemed strangely preoccupied. As soon as they had finished, he rang for the dishes to be cleared and, when that was achieved, started to shrug himself into his many-caped coat.

"Where are you going?" asked Alice in dismay.

"Out. Haunting. I must find you a house."

"I shall come with you."

"Ah, no, that you will not. You will stay here and warm yourself at the fire and then put yourself to bed."

"It is only seven o'clock in the evening," said Alice, but he was already rummaging through the box of jewels and selecting some of the finest pieces. "Mayhap, I shall find a sale for these at this hour," he said, speaking more to himself than to Alice.

And then, quite suddenly, he was gone.

Alice looked wistfully at the spot where he had last been. Everything was being set in action—and so soon. She had hoped they might have at least one last evening together.

She began to consider what her life would be without him and felt filled with dread. She would have a household and an army of servants to rule. She would have some female companion to launch her into the terrifying society of London, a companion who might one day see beneath the thin disguise of French aristocrat, to the shivering scullery maid underneath.

And what if the ghost's identity were discovered? Did they still burn witches?

Alice moved over to an easy chair beside the fire and tried to relax, but frightened thought after frightened thought chased around in her brain.

Fretting and anxious and worried, she waited until two in the morning, but still he did not return.

At last, tired out, she undressed and chose one of the bedrooms and wearily climbed into bed.

Outside lay smoky London, unknown, menacing . . . and lonely.

FOUR

"**My dear Alice,** you must be guided by me. Your uncle commanded me to mould your taste. How are we to impress the *ton* an you don't do as I say?" said Miss Emily Snapper intensely.

Alice turned slowly in front of the looking glass and stared at her reflection with resignation. "If you say so," she rejoined in a dead voice. Privately Alice thought the lemon-colored sarsenet dress trimmed with a vast quantity of artificial roses and white lace drapery and fastened down the front with topaz snaps, too fussy and aging. Her once glossy black hair was teased and frizzled into a top-heavy style. But, as in all other things, she knew that her companion, Miss Snapper, would have the last word.

Alice was preparing to depart for the opening ball of the London Season, to be held at the Duchess of Courtland's town house in Gloucester Square. For Alice, Comtesse de la Valle-Chenevix was accepted everywhere. The redoubtable Miss Snapper had seen to that.

Alice had hardly seen the Duke in the last seven days before he had disappeared for good. He had arranged the rental of a pretty house in Manchester Square, banked a great deal of money for her, arranged a man of business for her, servants were hired, furnishings bought and, finally, the formidable Miss Snapper hired as companion.

Miss Snapper was of the untitled aristocracy and came from an impoverished Surrey family which the Duke had known in their palmy days of the last century, and had felt obliged to supply a home to this last relic of the family. In that she knew everyone and was acceptable everywhere, was beyond question. The Duke had in his whirlwind of activity failed to notice that she was too intense and managing a spinster to be companion to such a young and such a green girl.

To Alice, it seemed as if she were never allowed to be alone with him. Miss Snapper was always present. She was a thin, angular woman in her thirties with a bony chest, snapping black eyes, a thin mouth which covered a row of sharp little teeth, dusty red hair and a conversational style which consisted of a series of denouncements.

She adored the Duke with an almost embarrassing passion of which he was quite oblivious, and any time Alice shyly tried to hint that she might like to be alone with her uncle, Miss Snapper would bare her sharp little teeth and simper, "Why, Alice dear. You are so quiet, I declare I cannot hear a word you say. Now you must run along and leave us old people to discuss your future."

And so, Alice's timid and awkward farewell to her "uncle" was made under the avid stare of Miss Snapper. For nights, she had cried to him with all her mind to come back but as the shadows lengthened, no shimmering figure came through the wall, no light mocking drawl came to her ears, and her eyes grew dull and heavy with nights of crying.

There had been, at one time, a real Lady Alice de la Valle-Chenevix, that Alice knew, for the Duke had gone to great lengths to furnish her with an authentic background. The family had been wiped out in the terrors of the French Revolution, with the exception of a baby girl who had gone unaccountably missing. He had coached Alice well in the history of her "family," and she had been prepared for all questions.

But the members of society she had so far met had accepted her at face value and were totally uninterested in her background. At first, she had found it hard to maintain a French accent morning, noon and night, but soon it became her natural speech and her accent was pronounced "charming" by the forgiving *ton* who had every reason to hate the French—for weren't they at war with the monsters?

On the day the Duke had left, the news of Wellington's victory at Ciudad Rodrigo had resounded through the streets. While Napoleon had turned his attention to Russia, the great Duke of Wellington had won this major battle, thereby kicking open the door into Spain which was held by Napoleon's vast armies. England had gone mad with joy at the news. The mail coaches outside the General Post Office in Lombard Street had been decked with laurels and flowers, oak leaves and ribbons and had gone thundering out through the trunk roads of England to bear the glad news to every corner.

At Vauxhall, rousing songs like "Hearts of Oak" and "Scots Wha' Hae" sounded in the night air. Napoleon no longer seemed the omnipotent ogre he had appeared in the years before when it had seemed at one time that he would surely land in England, and nurses had terrified the children to sleep, singing:

"Baby, baby, naughty baby,
Hush you squalling thing, I say;
Hush your squalling, or it may be
Bonaparte may pass this way.

"Baby, baby, he's a giant,
Tall and black as Rouen steeple;

And he dines and sups, rely on't,
Every day on naughty people."

But Alice was as uninterested in the war as she had been when she had toiled in the kitchens of the Hall. She read a great deal whenever she could and, then, in the evenings, dully allowed herself to be dressed like a doll by the energetic Miss Snapper and promenaded to breakfasts and *fêtes champêtre* and Venetian dinners and routs, each one seeming the same to Alice.

Her lack of interest in London society made her seem a very aloof little aristocrat. She was not besieged with admirers desirous of dancing with her as she sat meekly beside Miss Snapper and dreamed away the evenings thinking of her lost Duke.

Her skin had lost its translucence, and her step, its spring. She danced heavily, often treading on her partner's toes and not even being aware she was doing so.

London cobbled, odoriferous, and yet the acme of ordered and mannered beauty, was the stage across which Alice numbly floated. Controlled since the Great Fire by Building Acts which laid down the ceiling heights, types of materials and numbers of stories to be used in every class of street, London spread out in street after street of exquisitely proportioned houses of brown and gray brick with their unadorned faces of freestone sash, the same neat white pillars on either side of their pedimented doors.

It had been a long hard winter followed by a brief, icy, squally spring.

At long last, on this very eve of the London Season, the weather had decided to favor the top ten thousand by turning warm and balmy. A pale green sky stretched high above Manchester Square. In hundreds of bedrooms nearby, young ladies were getting ready to plunge into the Marriage Market and emerge with a husband. What other ambition was there for a properly brought up young miss? Orchestras tuned up, hothouse flowers were banked against walls, elegant suppers prepared, flambeaux lit—and hearts trembled with excitement as girls armed themselves for the all-important battle to come with all their weapons at the ready—fan, smelling salts and seductive smile.

But for Alice, each evening as the blue shadows gathered at the end of the streets and the lamplighter made his rounds with his oil can, was another little death, as night after night she lost hope that he would come.

She felt sad and tired and badly dressed and Miss Snapper irritated her beyond reason. Now the fact that Miss Snapper was beginning to irritate the meek Alice should have been a sign to the girl that she was slowly coming back to life. But she was unaware of this and simply began to tap her foot as Miss Snapper's intense voice grated in her ears.

"You must *sparkle* a little more, Alice. You want animation. You should not be vulgar, of course, and put yourself forward. Your so dear uncle would agree with me, I am sure. We both know what is best for you."

"My uncle," said Alice with a rare flash of spirit, "would not approve of your calling me by my Christian name instead of my title."

Miss Snapper studied this spark of rebellion with avid interest and then proceeded to stamp it out.

"Tish, child," she cried, tripping forward and winding one long bony arm around Alice's waist. "Are we not the dearest of friends? Don't I dote on you? You are frightened because it is the opening ball of the Season. But you shall come about. Let us descend to the drawing room and await the carriage. What think you of my gown?"

"Very fine," said Alice in a flat voice. She actually thought it would surely be better if they exchanged gowns, Miss Snapper's sprig muslin being more suited to a young girl, and Alice's ornate ballgown being more flattering on a woman of mature years and sallow complexion.

As they descended the elegant curved staircase into the small tiled hall, and thence through into the green and gold drawing room with its fashionably backless sofas and striped upholstery, Alice suddenly felt something strange happening to her mind. It was as if a great black weight of despair had been lifted from it. All at once, she knew her ghost was dead to her, that he no longer thought of her. She felt empty and light, a feeling which persisted right to the august doors of the Duchess of Courtland's town house where the flambeaux hissed and flared in their iron brackets against the wall.

Alice was vividly aware of being alive, vividly conscious of each sight and scent, of the splendor of the gowns and jewels, of the tantalizingly sweet strains of a waltz drifting across the warm air.

She was young and would be pretty again once she had crept from under the domineering shadow of her companion. There were many handsome men about. Why had she not noticed them before?

Alice sat sedately enough beside Miss Snapper, but her large eyes had begun to sparkle and there was a delicate blush on her cheeks.

"I say, said Lord Harold Webb, raising his quizzing glass, "ain't that the little Frenchie who was at Haversham's ball?"

His friend, Harold Russell, followed his gaze and then sniggered. "Damme, if it ain't," he said cheerfully. "Pon rep, you was bosky that night. Said to me she and her friend melted through the wall."

"Stow it," said Webb brutally, an angry expression marring his handsome features. "Pretty little chit, all the same. Tell you what. Ask her for a dance. Bound to be impressed."

Lord Harold Webb was very handsome, being fair with dark brown eyes and a high complexion. He was tall and well built and his clothes had been tailored by the hand of a master. He had been complimented on his good looks since the day he was born. He was possessed of a handsome fortune and he delighted in the pleasures of the London Season, for he knew he was much sought after. The fact that men, with the exception of his unlovely friend Mr. Russell, did not seem to seek his company much, held no sway with the ladies who appeared to adore him one and all.

He had several times been on the point of popping the question but had always drawn back at the last minute. For the lady of his choice always seemed ... well ... too independent and not conscious enough of the great favor that he was about to bestow on her.

Mr. Russell's restless gaze had swung away from Alice, but Webb continued to stare. Alice looked up and saw his eye, hideously enlarged by the quizzing glass, glaring at her from the other side of the ballroom and gave an involuntary chuckle.

That was when Harold Webb moved forward to ask her to dance.

Relieved of the depression which had been darkening her days, Alice danced as lightly as she had at the ball with the Duke, and talked just as lightly in her charming French accent. She did not hear a word Lord Harold addressed to her. She was pleasurably conscious of the envious glances she was receiving from the other debutantes and experienced a heady feeling of success for the first time.

"Making a cake of yourself over Frenchie," sneered Mr. Russell when Webb had at last reluctantly surrendered Alice to her next partner.

"Her name," said Webb stiffly, "is Alice, Comtesse de la Valle-Chenevix and I'll thank you to refer to that gel with respect in future, Harry."

"So! Here we go again," laughed Harry. "All set for the altar and then you get cold feet at the last minute. I don't see me ever being your best man. What's so special about this Comtesse? Them French émigrés are ten a penny."

"She has a feminine sweetness unusual in our modern gel," said Webb pompously. "The lady I would wish to be my wife should be someone pliant, who could be moulded . . ."

"Bullied, rather," said Harry.

"Nonsense. Everyone knows the male is the superior sex. Women with too much to say for themselves do not make good wives."

"Funny how the female of the species don't seem to have got hold of that idea," mocked Harry. "Your Comtesse may have other interests."

"Other than me?" said Lord Harold, his

fine eyes sparkling with amazement. "My dear chap, no woman wishes for any other man an she is blessed with my company."

That did, in fact, seem to be the case, although Harry thought to himself that no woman had really been in his friend's company long enough to find the pompous ass who lay underneath that handsome exterior. Harry did not really like Lord Harold Webb, but one had to have a companion, and no one else seemed anxious to fill that role.

Alice's newfound animation had attracted more than Lord Harold Webb to her side, and Miss Snapper sat with the chaperones and watched Alice with flat, black eyes. It was the first time that Miss Snapper had been made to feel the paid companion she actually was, for usually a very meek and mild Alice sat at her side throughout the evening, only rarely being asked to dance.

"She is become too bold," thought Miss Snapper. "I must speak to her very sternly."

Miss Snapper's restive mind turned to Alice's uncle, as it frequently did. He had not said he would return, but surely he would visit London again some time to see how his niece fared. He had said he planned to make an extended stay on the Continent, but what French anti-Bonapartist wanted to be anywhere on the Continent at such a time?

A little smile played around Miss Snapper's thin lips. She felt sure a certain attraction had sprung up between herself and Alice's uncle. Now, if Alice were to become married, Miss Snapper would lose her position. But, her busy mind raced, Alice would need his permission to marry, and surely he would return for the wedding. Miss Snapper closed her eyes and gave herself up to a blissful dream of Alice's wedding where she, Miss Snapper, would stand beside Alice's uncle, the Comte, receiving the guests. "This marriage has put ideas in my head, Miss Snapper," he whispered, pressing her hand in a feverish grip. By the time Miss Snapper emerged from this particular dream, she was convinced that Alice's uncle had been well and truly smitten with the fair Miss Snapper and had not received enough encouragement.

Alice was dancing with Harold Webb a second time and they seemed to be getting along famously.

"Ye . . . e . . . es," thought Miss Snapper, observing the couple through narrowed eyes. "A marriage. That is what is needed to bring him home."

It was with pleasure that Miss Snapper, therefore, gave Webb permission to take Alice driving at the fashionable hour next day. It was with less pleasure that she discovered she had a rebel on her hands. Webb was due to call for Alice at five in the afternoon. Miss Snapper, rising late, discovered that Alice had left much earlier with her lady's maid to go shopping.

She fretted and fumed until Alice returned, her carriage laden with parcels.

"What have you done?" cried Miss Snapper as two footmen carried in the parcels. "Such extravagance! What your dear uncle would . . ."

"I have no time to talk to you, Miss Snapper," said Alice firmly. "I am awaiting the court hairdresser, Monsieur Antoine. *Tiens!* How red your face has become, Miss Snapper. A *soupçon* less rouge, I pray."

And with that Alice swept on up the stairs, leaving Miss Snapper glaring impotently after her.

But Emily Snapper was not easily defeated. Taking a deep breath, she mounted the stairs to Alice's bedroom and stared in dismay at the array of silks and satins spread about the room. "That is not all, madam," said Alice gaily. "The rest, they come later. The ones that are being made specially."

"You must give me your uncle, the Comte's direction," said Miss Snapper firmly. "He would not approve. Only see this gown! It is nigh transparent."

"It is, how you say, all the crack," said Alice. "But it is useless asking me for *mon oncle's* direction since I do not know. I can furnish you, however, with the name and address of my man of business, Monsieur Bower. He will assure you I have sole control of my fortune."

Miss Snapper thought rapidly and decided

a strategic retreat vas best. She would catch young Alice when she was in a more vulnerable mood.

Alice heard ε closing of the door and sighed with relief. She was sure her small stock of courage had been about to run out. She could not believe she had already been so brave. But she was to drive out with the handsomest man in London. She would be the envy of the ladies of the *ton* and young Alice was human enough to relish that idea.

At precisely five o'clock, she descended the stairs, wearing a sprigged muslin gown with small puffed sleeves and deep flounces at the hem. Her long black hair had been cut *à la victime* and the saucy crop made her face seem more piquant and her eyes larger and brighter.

Seemingly oblivious to Miss Snapper's disapproving silence, she tied a chip straw bonnet on her head and picked up a lacy parasol as Lord Harold Webb's high perch phaeton drew up outside the door.

Hyde Park at the fashionable hour was a wonderful spectacle. Glossy horses, silks and laces, taffeta and feathers, uniforms and quizzing glasses and curving top hats. The warm sun blazed down on the high gloss of the carriages, on the spun glass wigs of the coachmen, on the rich color and embroidery of hammer cloths. Clouds of dust sailed up into the summer air making the whole moving, shifting scene seem unreal, as if the whole panorama were being viewed through gauze.

Webb's voice was like music in Alice's ears. He told her what should be worn in society and what should not be worn. He told her that Mr. Brummell, that famous leader of fashion, was nothing more than a popinjay. That the Prince Regent was a disgrace to the country and his extravagences were shocking, and that he, Harold Webb, had told his Royal Highness just that.

"Fact!" he declared, under Alice's awed stare. "Walked right up to him at Carlton House t'other day and I said, 'Prinny,' I said, 'You're a disgrace.' "

"Weren't you afraid?" breathed Alice.

"Pooh!" he said, deftly edging his phaeton through the press. "A Webb is never afraid."

A shadow crossed Alice's little face. "Not even of ghosts?" she asked in a low voice.

"No," he said stoutly. "And Harold Webb can tell you why, for Harold Webb has seen one! Fact! With these here eyes."

"Please tell me," said Alice urgently. Oh, the relief of finding she was not alone with her phantoms!

"Well, it was like this," he said, vastly pleased at her interest. He reined in under a stand of trees and settled back slightly to make the most of it.

"I was at Lord Framont's place, down Surrey way, with my friend, Mr. Russell. Deuced old barn of a place it was. Very damp. Harry—

that's my friend, Mr. Russell—he says, he says we would catch the ague. 'Webbs never catch the ague,' says I. 'Place is bound to be haunted,' says he. 'There ain't no such thing as ghosts,' says I. But one night after we'd been playing piquet with Framont and some friends, we didn't finish until the small hours and Harry—that's my friend, Mr. Russell, the thin chappie who was at the ball t'other night—and I shared a candle up to bed. All of sudden, there comes this great wailing. 'What the devil'—beg pardon, Countess—says Harry, that's Mr. Russell, my friend, 'is that?' 'Fore the words were out of his mouth, this great thing all in a cursed sheet and chains and things, comes flying across the room. Harry—that's my friend—he turns as pale as things. But me, now I'm a Webb, and us Webbs don't take count of anything, no matter which side of the grave it's on.

" 'Get thee hence,' says I, 'cos I'd read that somewhere in a vastly entertaining book and that's the sort of thing one says to ghosts according to this book, that is. And Harry—Mr. Russell—he says, 'By George! You've done it. It worked!' And as sure as I'm standing here—hem, sitting here, it had!"

"I wasn't thinking of that kind of ghost," said Alice sadly. Almost involuntarily her mind reached out, trying one more time to call her ghost, but there was nothing there, nothing at all.

He leaned forward and pressed her hand. "I

have frightened you with my talk of ghosts," he said softly. Alice blushed rosily, taken aback by the unexpected familiarity and delighted at the same time to have this extremely handsome man paying court to her.

"I had better take you back to the crowd," he said, looking down at her roguishly, "or I shall quite forget myself. I was saying to Harry—that's my friend—only t'other night. I said, 'That Comtesse is a deuced fine gel!' There! That's what I said," declared Webb, noticing with great complacency, the ebb and flow of blood mantling Alice's cheeks.

Harold Webb was always plagued with a nagging fear that one day he might "lose his touch," that he might no longer be able to make a pretty girl blush and tremble.

As he tooled his carriage back to the throng, he kept giving Alice little sidelong glances. She was almost beautiful, he decided. Quite the way she looked when he had first seen her.

"That fellow with the yaller hair," he said abruptly. "Friend of yours?"

"I'm afraid I don't . . ." began Alice.

"The one at Wadham Hall."

Alice went very still, very rigid. *"Alors, m'sieu,"* she said slowly, her French accent very marked. "I fear you are mistake."

"No. No. It *was* you," said Lord Harold. "At the Christmas ball."

Alice almost visibly relaxed. "Oh, that was

my uncle, Gervase. He is on the Continent *en ce moment.*"

"Y'know," he went on, "talking of ghosts. 'Fraid I must have had too much to drink at that ball. I could have sworn, you and that uncle vanished right into the wall." He leaned back and roared with laughter, oblivious that Alice had turned quite pale.

Alice suddenly longed for the security of that little secret room and then banished the thought resolutely from her mind. Those days were gone, never to return. She was young and rich and free and the handsomest man in London was paying court to her.

Now, had Alice been more alive on all suits, she would undoubtedly have found Webb a crashing bore, but she had only been used to the conversation of the kitchens and, until the evening before, had not much listened to what anyone said on her social outings in London. Her witty ghost, she discounted, because he was a sort of god to her and she did not expect any mortal to achieve his magnificent standards.

And so it was a very grateful Alice who allowed herself to be courted by Webb. An Alice, so grateful, that she did not realize she had blossomed into a great beauty. She could not quite throw off the yoke of Miss Snapper's bullying and derogatory remarks although she stuck grimly to her own mode of dress.

"It will not be much longer anyway," thought Alice one day, "for I am going to be married and have children and one day I shall have the courage to go to my poor ghost's grave and lay flowers on his tomb." For Alice now firmly believed the Duke had returned from whence he had come. On Sundays, while Miss Snapper murmured a litany of prices of various bonnets beside her in the pew, Alice prayed for the soul of the Duke.

And then, it seemed inevitably, Webb proposed and Alice accepted. Miss Snapper was in seventh heaven. Her dream was about to come true. She had been very gentle with Alice of late as that picture of herself and the Comte receiving Alice's wedding guests, grew clearer.

Carefully, Miss Snapper considered her own background. She was one of the Snappers of Surrey and she was the last of that noble line. That the Snappers had never distinguished themselves in any field whatsoever was something of which she was very proud. Only vulgar people brought themselves to the notice of the many-headed.

She thought it odd however that Webb had not asked her permission to pay his addresses and could not refrain from saying as much.

"My uncle signed papers before he left," said Alice, "allowing me complete control of my affairs—not only my monetary affairs, but my marital affairs."

Miss Snapper cast down her eyes to hide the bitter disappointment and resentment in them. She badly needed this job, for her family had fallen on hard times before her father's death. But to see Alice so glowing, so happy, so *uncle-less*, was infuriating, to say the least.

That this little French chit should have so much while she, Emily Snapper, sprung from one of England's oldest families, had nothing, was a thought which planted the seeds of burgeoning hate.

She longed for a weapon but never did she think for one moment that it would be Lord Harold who put it into her hands.

He called one day while Alice was out with her maid expressly to see Miss Snapper and, as that lady listened eagerly, the problem was soon explained.

Alice and her dashing clothes and smart hair crop was *hem*, attracting too much deuced attention. He wanted his wife to be modest and well, don't you see, more the way she had been when he had seen her at the opening ball of the Season.

"Leave it to me," said Miss Snapper, patting Lord Harold's hand with her own bony one, encased in a lace mitten.

"Is Alice expected soon?" asked Webb.

"She should be back in half an hour," said Miss Snapper. "That gives us time to discuss a little plan of campaign . . ."

Alice, very flushed and beautiful, sailed in some forty minutes later from her walk and then stood, quite still, surveying her fiancé and Miss Snapper. Miss Snapper had a little curved smile pinned on her mouth, and Webb was staring at the toe of one polished boot.

He did not even rise to his feet.

"What is the matter?" asked Alice. "Has something gone wrong?"

Webb continued to stare at the toe of his boot.

"Sit down, my love," said Miss Snapper, patting the edge of the striped sofa next to her. "Lord Harold Webb and I have just been talking about you."

"Tiens!" said Alice. "I would have thought Harold would have had the courtesy to speak to me about anything that worried him."

"There are times when the advice of an older woman is needed," said Miss Snapper smugly. She had not enjoyed herself so much in weeks. "Now, I have told you Alice, that your mode of dress and behavior leave much to be desired. You would not listen to me. Perhaps you will listen to Lord Harold Webb."

Alice sat down nervously on the sofa and looked inquiringly at the handsome face of her fiancé.

"Alice," he said heavily. "There is something about you that is not ... well ... quite ... well, hem ... your behavior is not that of a lady."

Alice, the scullery maid, crouched on the sofa, half putting up a hand as if to ward off a blow.

Webb saw her cringe and that excited him in a pleasurable way. "Yes," he went on in a more assured manner. "I wish to take you to meet my parents this weekend. They are surprised that I should consider marrying a foreigner. They will be even more surprised if they find I am escorting a *fast* female."

"What is up with my appearance?" demanded Alice, fighting to regain some of her spirit.

"It pains me to say this," said Webb, getting to his feet and coming to stand over her. "There is something a trifle common in your bearing."

How Alice trembled. The modish Alice fled and the servant came back. "Mr. Brummell, he said I was the *daintiest* creature," she ventured.

"Pah! *Brummell!*" said Webb in accents of loathing.

Alice was by now too crushed to protest. She had been so sure she looked all the crack. Had her style only been that of a kitchen maid?

"Miss Snapper will select your wardrobe for your forthcoming visit. Now, if I may have a word in private with my fiancée, Miss Snapper? . . ."

Emily Snapper rose reluctantly. She did not want to leave them alone together in case Alice persuaded Webb to accept her as she was. But Webb was already holding open the door for her.

When Miss Snapper had left, Webb came forward and took both Alice's hands in his own and raised her to her feet. She really looked deuced pretty, he reflected. Too pretty by half. He had been acutely aware, as Alice had not, that she was already attracting a great deal of warm attention from the gentlemen of the *ton*. And he liked her like this, cringing and beaten and humble.

He caught her in his arms and pressed his mouth hard against her own. Alice's tired mind registered that her lord had had garlic at some point earlier in the day, small beer and eggs, but apart from that, she felt no stirring of the senses.

"There!" he said triumphantly drawing back. "You must not faint from excess of emotion," he added kindly, although Alice was standing, quite rigid, and never had any woman looked less like falling down in a faint.

"I shall call for you on Friday, my love," he added. "Now, you will obey Miss Snapper for my sake. It is the duty of a wife to obey her husband implicitly. Do you know that?"

"Yes, Harold," whispered Alice. Oh, she must change her ways and do as they say lest they guess her guilty secret.

The late Duke of Haversham had not returned to the grave. He was in fact very much alive—if a ghost can be said to be alive. He had found his days extremely lonely without Alice and had found himself thinking of her constantly. But, he told himself sternly she would have to make a life without him,

95

else how could she achieve a successful marriage? Then he wondered why these noble and altruistic thoughts left him so depressed. Finally he was almost able to put her completely from his mind. At times, he felt uneasily that she was in trouble and calling him, but he built a mental brick wall against her pleas in his mind. The sooner she forgot about him, the better. He had not visited the present Duke since the night he had lectured his successor on the evil of his ways.

Haunting had lost its savor. He traveled far and wide from the Hall, ranging over the country at night. At last, he decided to settle down in the secret room and write his memoirs. For once, he was relatively content, and the only thing that occasionally marred his nights was a longing to see the light of day again. But try as he could, he could not materialize after the first cock crowed and the sky paled in the east.

And then one night when he was raiding the kitchen after all the servants were abed, he saw a newspaper lying on the table in the butler's pantry.

Idly he picked it up and popped it on the tray next to his evening meal. He drifted over to the wall and, as he did so, he noticed that the paper was open at the social column. The next minute the black type seemed to leap out of the page and scream at him that Alice, Comtesse de la Valle-Chenevix, was engaged to Lord Harold Webb. He lost his concentration and walked slap bang into the wall, and the contents of the tray spun out off over the kitchen and fell with a horrendous crash.

He rubbed his forehead in a dazed way, picked up the newspaper as he heard the sound of approaching feet, and melted through the wall—this time successfully—and drifted upward through the floors to the secret room.

The Duke lit the candles and sat down at the table, spreading the newspaper carefully out in front of him. There was no doubt about it. Alice was engaged.

He looked at the date at the top. The paper was two weeks old.

Well, this is what he had wanted for the girl. She was only a scullery maid and now she was marrying a Lord. She had done very well for herself.

He turned his concentration wholly on his memoirs, becoming so absorbed that he even forgot to eat He put aside his manuscript with a sigh and looked at the clock on the mantle. Nearly dawn. He had not much of a life in summer, he reflected wryly.

And then, quite clearly, like a bell in his brain, he heard her calling him heard Alice calling for help

He started to his feet—and groaned. A glimmer of livid gray was spreading along the horizon He could do nothing until night came again

When he awoke the next evening, or came to, or materialized—he was never quite sure how to describe the phenomenon of his re-birth to himself—he did not at first remember Alice, but was instantly plagued with a nagging feeling of unease. Then his eye fell on the newspaper, still lying on the table, and he remembered. Alice. Engagement. Her cry for help.

The Duke quickly dressed in evening clothes, missing for the first time, Jamieson, his valet of the old days who could surely have dealt with all these difficult, modern styles of hair-dressing. "It was easier in my day," he mused. "I could simply wear a wig. Of course, many still do, but I was never *démodé* in my time, and I do not intend to be in this."

As he floated swiftly over the countryside, his fears for Alice had begun to recede. He should not have left her alone so soon. She had probably found it extremely difficult to accustom herself to society. Perhaps she had forgotten her French accent.

When he arrived at Alice's house it was to be met with the intelligence that Alice and Miss Snapper were visiting Webb's parents' home. Webb's parents were the Earl and Countess of Markhampton. Their home lay a few miles outside Tunbridge Wells.

The Duke was thankful that he had passed his early days since he had left Alice, travel-ing extensively over the countryside. He had become adept at finding his way about the sky and espying familiar landmarks on the ground at night, particularly on a fine starry night like this one.

The black, straggly mass of the town of Tunbridge Wells was soon reached and then he veered east, searching for Runley Manor, Webb's parents' home.

At long last he found himself above it. He wondered if they kept country hours but, as he sank lower, he saw that the windows of the Manor were ablaze with lights and there seemed to be a ball in progress in a great room on the ground floor.

The long windows were open to the night air. He floated gently down and stood on the shaven grass of the lawn. He decided to watch Alice first. He did not want to startle her by approaching her. He moved quietly up the terrace steps and eased himself through the windows, standing partly concealed by the curtain.

At first he did not recognize her—and then all at once she was almost in front of him. She looked happy and animated although the Duke, putting up his quizzing glass, could not quite believe the fussiness of her dress or the clumsiness of her hairstyle. Alice was dancing with a fresh-faced young man in an ill-fitting suit. They were waltzing and he seemed to be dancing on her toes most of the time, but he looked easy and amiable. The Duke thought this must be Lord Harold Webb. Well, he was not the most elegant of creatures but he looked a good-hearted soul. He would do very well.

The Duke was torn between leaving immediately now that he had found Alice in good spirits, or staying to give her a lecture on the dowdiness of her dress.

It was then he noticed the shadows under her eyes and that her eyes themselves were suspiciously puffy.

He stayed, his bright blue gaze fixed on her every movement. The waltz finished at last and Alice began to promenade with her partner as was the custom. Suddenly, a tall, very handsome man with a rather pompous face came up to Alice accompanied by Miss Snapper. Miss Snapper seemed to say a few short sharp words at which Alice flushed miserably and stared at the floor. Her unresisting hand was taken from her partner's arm and placed by Miss Snapper firmly on that of the handsome young man who led Alice off to the side of the ballroom, talking fiercely in an undertone and, to the Duke's horror, he caught the glint of tears in Alice's eyes.

It was time to make his appearance. He sauntered across the ballroom floor in Miss Snapper's direction, examining the companion as if for the first time and not liking what he saw.

Her gown, he noticed, was extremely rich and around her scrawny neck was a ruby necklace which he recognized as having belonged to his late wife.

"Monsieur Le Comte!" gasped Miss Snapper as the Duke appeared before her. "We had not heard . . . did not expect you . . ."

Her thin hand flew to the necklace at her throat.

"Where is this Lord Harold Webb?" said the Duke sternly.

"Ah, he is flirting with Alice and us old things should not intrude," said Miss Snapper, flirting horribly with her fan.

"Madam," said the Duke awfully, "I am not yet in my dotage although you may be. I find your personal remarks offensive in the extreme. You forget yourself. Pray, present me to my niece this instant."

Miss Snapper quailed under his icy gaze. The pleasurable bullying of Alice in which she had so freely indulged was going to be discovered unless she could have a word with Alice first in private and threaten her into silence.

"Indeed, yes, milord," she murmured, ducking her head in a nervous gesture. "Pray wait here. I will return with Alice."

The Duke stood by the side of the ballroom floor, staring about him with interest. The Earl of Markhampton appeared to be wealthy. The room was decorated with fine silk hangings of green and gold.

Hundreds of the most expensive scented candles perfumed the air. Hothouse flowers and palms were placed around the perimeter of the floor, and from the supper room came the delectable aroma of good French cooking. He was just thinking that Miss Snapper was taking an unconscionable time about bringing Alice to him when a latecomer entered the ballroom and he raised his quizzing glass and let out a sigh of pure appreciation. A beautiful blonde had entered with her chaperone. Her hair owed all to art but was magnificent for all that. It gleamed like burnished brass in the candlelight and her enameled face was a flawless oval. She had a wicked pair of black eyes, a diaphanous gown which was dampened to the point of indecency and, wonder upon wonders, her toenails were painted gold!

He straightened his waistcoat and headed purposefully toward her.

And so it was that Alice, entering the ballroom with Webb anchored firmly to one side and Miss Snapper to the other, saw her "uncle" for the first time since he had left her that winter's night. He was smiling down into the eyes of a bold blonde and seemed to have forgotten the existence of everyone and everything else.

Miss Snapper gave a malicious titter. "You see how happy your uncle is?" she said. "He is content to leave you in our good care. We have your best interests at heart, Alice. You must tell him you lent me this pretty necklace."

"But I didn't!" exclaimed Alice.

"*Say* you did," hissed Miss Snapper. "I know he admired it and he would not like to think you ungenerous to your poor companion. Only vulgar people are cruel and mean."

Alice winced. Miss Snapper had found she could get Alice to agree to practically anything provided she told the girl that things were "vulgar." Alice lived in fear that Miss Snapper would discover her humble origins, not knowing that Miss Snapper merely thought Alice, being French—and who wanted to be French? —was taken up with the idea of becoming the perfect English lady.

Poor Alice numbly watched the Duke as he flirted outrageously.

She wanted to run to him and tear him away from that blonde harpy. She wanted to cry to him that she was lonely and hurt and lost, that she had made a terrible mistake, that Webb and Miss Snapper were bullying the life out of her.

But the heartless ghost philandered on, and at last Alice could bear it no longer and begged to be allowed to retire.

Miss Snapper and Lord Harold cheerfully agreed. There would be no confrontation with Alice's uncle that night.

When Miss Snapper had seen Alice safely to her room, she descended the stair to the ballroom where she found Webb awaiting her.

"I think, my dear Miss Snapper," said Webb in measured tones, "that we must plan. Come with me!"

Her hurt at the Duke's snub abating under

the interest of this newfound intrigue, Miss Snapper eagerly followed him.

He led her into a small anteroom and closed the door. The faint strains of a lilting Scottish reel filtered faintly into the quiet room.

"I do not think, Miss Snapper," said Webb pompously, "that our little Alice will be able to refrain from telling her uncle that we have been . . . hem . . . a trifle rough with her. It was all for her own good but he may not see it that way and may forbid the marriage."

"He cannot." said Miss Snapper eagerly. "Alice told me he had left her papers allowing her to marry whom she chooses."

"Well, she may use his support to cancel the engagement. Alice has not been happy of late," said Webb. He spoke the truth. His daily hectoring criticism had reduced Alice to a quaking wreck. But Webb found Alice, shaking and frightened, infinitely exciting and did not want her any other way.

Miss Snapper lowered her eyes. "It could be, mayhap, that he might find it necessary to give his blessing to the marriage . . ."

"You mean? . . . She will not allow me intimacies and it did not seem to me necessary to press my suit since we are shortly to be wed."

Miss Snapper fidgeted with the lace of her mittens. "There are ways it could be achieved."

The reel finished with a crashing chord and the faint murmur of voices permeated the room and Lord Harold looked down at the companion with an unpleasant smile on his face.

"You hate her, don't you?" he said.

Miss Snapper raised her black eyes to the ceiling. "As God is my witness, my lord, I have only the girl's best interests at heart."

"Oh whatever way you want it," he sneered. "How is this seduction to be achieved without her screaming the place down?"

"I never said . . ."

"Oh, yes you did in your own sweet way. Stow the hypocrisy."

Miss Snapper cast down her eyes again. Her hand flew nervously to the jewels at her neck. She had been feathering her nest very well and unless she quickly swallowed her pride, then Alice might escape.

"She has not been sleeping well," she said. "Some chloral in her milk . . ."

"Do it now," he said urgently, "I'll carry her to my bed and you tell . . . No, that will not answer. My servants will pretend to be shocked and will tell Alice's uncle that she is abed with me. You keep to your own quarters. Quickly."

Alice was tossing and turning on her bed when Miss Snapper crept into the room, a glass of hot milk in her hand. Alice was tormented by thoughts of the Duke holding that blonde hussy in his arms.

She had longed for him and dreamed of seeing him again through the long, lonely months and he had not even a thought to spare for her. Not that she was in love with him! That was ridiculous. She had looked on him as a sort of father or as the uncle he pretended to be. He was not kind. He was heartless. A philandering phantom who did not know that fair hair was desperately unfashionable. Alice looked up and found Miss Snapper bending over her and cringed against the pillows.

"Here is something to help you sleep," murmured Miss Snapper in a soothing voice.

"Milk," said Alice wretchedly. "I do not want milk."

"But it will help you sleep," urged Miss Snapper.

Sleep! Alice realized that was what she longed for more than anything. To die, to sleep, to blot out the wicked world and its bullies for a few hours.

She drank the milk while Miss Snapper watched her with satisfaction.

In the shadows in the corner of the room, the Duke watched also. He had been hidden in the walls of the anteroom where Miss Snapper and Webb had had their enlightening conversation.

He watched grimly as Alice collapsed quickly into a deep drugged sleep, watched as Miss Snapper signaled to someone unseen in the corridor, and then Webb entered and picked up Alice's slim body and carried her from the room.

The Duke quickly slid down through the

floor and placed himself in a prominent position in the hall where the last of the guests were leaving. Miss Snapper, meanwhile, retired quickly to her own modest room. Some thoughtful servant had left a glass of warm milk by *her* bed. Miss Snapper gave a thin smile. *It* wasn't drugged anyway. She picked it up and drank it down in one gulp and began to prepare herself for bed.

In *his* room, Webb placed Alice in his bed and slowly began to undress. The stage was set. By now his valet should be informing Alice's uncle of his niece's disgrace.

"What!" yelled the Duke in a great voice so that a few of the last guests and the Earl and Countess of Markhampton turned round in surprise. "My niece in bed with Lord Harold Webb! Is this what you encourage in your house?" he demanded of the Earl. "Seduction of innocent virgins?"

Without waiting to see the effect of his words, the Duke began to rapidly mount the stairs. The Earl and his guests hurried after, but as they reached the first landing, the Duke had mysteriously disappeared.

"Monsieur Le Comte moves quickly," said the Earl in surprise. He had been apprised of the identity of his new guest. "Nonetheless, I must find out the truth of this matter. My Harold would never do such a thing. It will all turn out to be a hum, mark my words!"

He hurried on with his wife behind him and his guests pressed close behind.

Lord Harold Webb heard the rumpus coming along the corridor and smiled. It was just as well he *wanted* to be discovered, he reflected smugly, or he would have had time to make things respectable long before they appeared. The room was in total darkness. Well, might as well get as much fun as possible. Alice was, after all, lying next to him. He thought of the feel of her warm body through the thin material of her nightgown when he had carried her to his bed and his pulses began to race.

He pulled the unconscious female body close to his own naked one, throwing the covers back first so that when Uncle Gervase burst in, he should have the maximum view.

He searched for the mouth beneath his in the dark. Just before the Earl and his party burst into the room, Lord Harold Webb was conscious of two bewildering physical sensations. Alice's mouth, instead of soft and childlike as he remembered, was hard and thin. And he had noticed she had lost weight of late, but never would have believed she could have possessed so many hard sharp bones.

Also just before the door opened, a branch of candles on the mantleshelf immediately sprang into flame as if by magic showing the stern and hard profile of Alice's Uncle Gervase. He was standing by the fireplace, looking toward the door.

"Good God!" cried the Earl bursting into

the room, "Oh, Harold, my son, what have you done?"

The guests crowded into the room behind him.

"This lady is my fiancée," said Harold, sitting up in bed with great unconcern. "I do not think we have done anything vastly wrong."

Then came the mocking voice of Uncle Gervase. "Alas! My poor Alice! To be cut out by a spinster."

Harold stared at the Duke who had turned and was lighting another branch of candles. He had a sudden sick feeling of dread. He turned slowly and looked down at the face lying on the pillow next to him.

Miss Snapper was lying, snoring. Her mouth was slightly open showing a glint of little, sharp teeth.

"There has been some terrible mistake," babbled Harold, pulling the bedclothes hurriedly about his naked body.

Now, the Duke had made sure that the drug he had put in Miss Snapper's milk was not very strong.

Under Lord Harold's horrified gaze, she slowly came awake. Her dazed eyes stared up into Webb's. Then she looked at the Earl and his guests, then at the Duke. And then she began to scream and scream and scream.

FIVE

Alice was alone in her drawing room in Manchester Square. She was lying on the sofa with her head buried in a new novel. She was completely and blissfully alone. No Miss Snapper. No sharp voices reprimanding her.

She was wearing a pretty sarsenet dress with a dozen flounces at the hem caught up in scallops. It had little puff sleeves and was fastened down the front with a row of little raised buttons. Her hair rioted about her head in artistic disorder. She had a little color in her cheeks. Her feet were comfortably encased in beaded slippers.

Alice put down her book and stared out at the fading light. She would not have much longer to wait.

It was two days since the ball, two whole

days since the Duke had cleverly terminated her engagement to Webb.

Alice smiled as she remembered the uproar which had greeted her when she had descended the stairs the next day.

The Earl of Markhampton was as pompous as his son, but for once that pomposity had been deflated. He had told her in hushed tones of the disgrace of his son. Harold, he had said, would have to marry Miss Snapper. She was a gentlewoman and had been compromised under his roof. Alice's uncle had left instructions that neither of the guilty couple was to approach his niece and that she was to pack her bags and return to London forthwith.

Alice, who did not yet know of the plot against her, could only assume that Webb had been nursing a secret passion for Miss Snapper all along. She did not know how miserable and trapped that young man now felt.

Neither Webb nor Miss Snapper could admit that it had been Alice who was supposed to be lying in his lordship's bed. But to Webb's horror, Miss Snapper, after she had recovered from her original screaming shock, had abruptly changed and had become the outraged maiden mixed with the coy virgin. For Miss Snapper's agile mind had quickly grasped the idea of an advantageous marriage. She was impoverished, but of good family.

Unaware of all this, Alice had listened

gravely to the Earl's apologies and had quietly gone away to order her servants to make ready to depart as soon as possible. She found it hard to conceal her joy.

On her first night home, the Duke had briefly appeared. He had been formal and aloof, only remaining long enough to tell her he was going to advertise for another companion. Alice had tried to protest but he had answered sternly that she could not live alone.

Now she was awaiting him again as she had waited so many times before. She rose from the sofa and crossed to the window, looking up hopefully at the steadily darkening sky and at the faraway twinkling of the first star.

She tripped over to the looking glass and patted her hair. All at once, she saw him behind her, his face reflected in the glass.

"I did not think phantoms could see their own image," she said, without turning round.

"A pox on all phantoms," said the ghost crossly. "I am tired of these short nights. It is not at all odd to me that I should see myself in the glass." He swiveled away from her and stared across the room at the open book lying on the sofa. "Novels! I thought as much. You have been reading rubbish."

Alice swung around, too happy to see him again to be angry with him. "I have ordered a late supper for us," she said. "I trust you have not dined."

"Don't be stupid," said the Duke nastily.

"How can I have dined when I have just materialized?"

"I forget, you see," said Alice apologetically. "You look so human."

He nodded his head, accepting the apology as his due. "Your servants will not be pleased at having to serve supper late," he said, taking a delicately enameled snuffbox from his pocket and opening the lid with a deft twist of his wrist.

"Oh, no, they are quite delighted," said Alice. "They are so pleased Miss Snapper is gone. I heard the chef tell the butler."

"Listening to servants' gossip, Alice?"

"Of course," said Alice. "I am a servant, remember."

"No, I will not remember," he said harshly. "I have gone to considerable pains to establish you as a lady of the *ton*. But if, in your sheer peasant ingratitude, you prefer to forget it, then that, my dear, is something you will have to overcome."

Tears started to Alice's eyes at the cold cruelty of his voice, but the butler was at the doorway announcing dinner.

The Duke imperiously held out his arm and she could do nothing but blink away the tears and try to swallow the lump in her throat.

It was a silent meal, Alice picking at her food and the Duke seemingly totally absorbed in making a hearty meal.

When the servants had at last retired, he

looked across the table at her. "I was hungry," he said.

Alice sighed. "Why does everyone bully me and snap at me so?"

"Because," said the Duke pouring himself a glass of port, "you have a cringing air about you, Alice, a very emanation of timidity which brings out the beast in people. You are eminently bullyable. You want spirit."

"How can I change?" wailed Alice.

"Oh, look in your glass," said the ghost testily. "You are a beautiful woman, Alice. Forget that scullery maid. She is as dead as . . . as I am."

"But there was no need for you to be so cross," said Alice in a low voice. "We have not really talked in so long. Have I done something to make you angry?"

"Have you done . . . ? Of course you have, you hen-witted brat. What on earth made you even consider wedding such a fool as Webb?"

"He was pleasant . . . at first," said Alice. "And he seemed so handsome. I was flattered that he should show an interest in me."

"Did he make love to you?"

"Yes," whispered Alice.

"You have lost your virginity," stated the Duke with contempt.

"NO!" shouted Alice, and then in a lower voice, "No, not that. He k-kissed me and f-fondled me."

"And that did pleasure you?"

"No," said Alice, raising her large eyes to look fully at him. "I felt nothing."

"I 'Faith, that was an excellent dinner," said the Duke cheerfully. "I do not know why I was so much at odds with the world. Come, dear child, we shall forget Webb and Snapper. They shall be the wicked phantoms of thy life—gone now to haunt thee no more. I have found a lady companion."

"Oh, dear," murmured Alice.

"I have taken care with this one. Nonetheless, it is for you to decide whether you want her. Her name is Cassandra Fadden. I shall tell you no more about her."

"Do you like my gown?" ventured Alice, not wishing to discuss this companion who would surely bully her.

"Stand up," he ordered, and when she complied, "Turn around."

He studied her thoughtfully for a long moment. "Pretty," he said at last. "Vastly pretty. Trust your own taste in clothes, child. You looked the veriest quiz under the tuition of the Snapper."

She flushed with pleasure and shyly resumed her chair and gathering all her small stock of courage she said, "Mayhap it would please you to stay in London with me for some days?"

"Mayhap it would," he drawled. "I have, however, started writing my memoirs. So far I am doing very well," he said with simple pride. "Whether anyone will believe them or not is another matter."

"Do you still wish me to get married?" asked Alice.

"What other future is there for you?" asked the Duke. "The money from the jewels will not last forever. You are young and healthy and normal. Of course you wish to have children and a home of your own."

"But my husband, he must never know my secret," said Alice. "How do you keep secrets from someone you love?"

"Well, you'd better learn to keep a still tongue in your head," he said acidly. "If you start babbling on about ghosts you'll end in Bedlam."

"I may not be able to fall in love with anyone suitable," pleaded Alice.

"What is love?" demanded the ghost, refilling his glass and settling down to a pleasurable dissertation. "It is frustrated lust, nothing more. What is marriage? Legalized lust. People fall in love because they do not know how to keep their lives simple. They have to go and mess it up by not only taking themselves too seriously but someone else as well. It is a bad basis for marriage for, after the first dizzy raptures are over, what do we find? A man and a woman, disillusioned and bored. That is what makes them seek extramarital affairs. That . . ."

"Stop!" cried Alice, putting her hands over her ears.

"I beg your pardon," said the Duke haughtily, "but I was in the middle of explaining one of my pet theories. You lack manners."

"Have you no heart?" cried Alice.

"Of course I have, you silly chit. I have that same organ that I took to the grave with me. It beats. It pumps blood. It did not fall in love when I was alive, so I think it is safe to assume it will not now I am dead. Now, where was I?"

"You were talking about disillusionment," said Alice in a dead voice. *"Tiens! Quelle bêtise!"*

"There is no need to be rude in French as well as English. Obviously you do not share my views. Yes, I shall stay with you for a few weeks. I think I should guide you in your choice of husband. There is not much to choose from here until the beginning of the Little Season but we shall do our best. While I am on the subject, it is not a good idea to let your swains kiss you and fondle you as you say young Webb did. Familiarities breed contempt. Keep a respectable distance until you are wed. It is strange to me to think of any man wishing to be intimate with you. Perhaps it is because I view you in the light of the niece you pretend to be. You are looking quite white and exhausted, my child. Do you wish to go to bed?"

"No," said Alice in a small voice.

"In that case we shall retire to the drawing room."

Alice meekly allowed herself to be led

through to the drawing room. She could not understand why she felt so sad and depressed. He was not going away. He was to stay with her. That was all she had longed and prayed for. Wasn't it?

"The night is chilly for summer," said the Duke. "I shall light a fire. Ah! I do not have to light my own fires anymore." He moved to ring the bell for a servant.

"Don't," said Alice. "I told the servants they could retire after we had finished our supper."

"Did you not think of my pleasure?" he demanded.

"I thought only of the servants," said Alice quietly. "It is not so long since I was one myself."

"And we are never, ever going to be allowed to forget it," snapped the Duke, bending over the fireplace and at the same time wondering why he was being so harsh with the girl. He busied himself lighting the fire while his mind turned over the problem. He decided it was the responsibility of taking care of Alice that irked. He came to the conclusion that his behavior was, however, at fault. And so in the manner of his kind of aristocrat, he decided to apologize sincerely and openly to Alice.

He swung around on his heels and smiled up at her. "I have been in the devil of a temper this evening," he said. "I think perhaps my spleen is disordered."

"Damn your spleen, sir!" cried Alice, "and damn you."

He stood up slowly and towered over her, his eyes like chips of blue ice. "You guttersnipe," he said, slowly and carefully enunciating each syllable. "I make you a handsome apology and all you can do is scream at me like a fishwife."

Alice stared at him, her wide eyes dark and amazed. "*That* was an apology!" she exclaimed. Then she buried her face in her hands and turned her back on him.

He stood looking at her in baffled rage. He noticed her shoulders were shaking and suddenly his rage died as quickly as it had sprung up.

The Duke moved forward and put his hands on her shoulders and turned her gently around, holding her slim shaking body against his own.

"There now," he said, tilting up her chin and then glaring down at her in amazement. For Alice was laughing—not crying as he had believed. Her bright eyes were sparkling and she was shaking with mirth. "Oh, y-you are s-so f-funny," she gasped when she could. "An apology, indeed."

The Duke held her a little away from him, looking down at her. All of a sudden a mocking smile lit up his blue eyes and he slowly pulled her close to him again and bent his head.

"No!" whispered Alice, closing her eyes.

She trembled against him, all laughter gone. She could feel his long fingers biting into her shoulders and smell the musky perfume he wore. Then one hand released one shoulder and came under her chin and pushed her head up and his lips met hers in a long exploring kiss, deeper and deeper and biting, parting her lips, his tongue sliding into her mouth, darting and searching. She felt her body burning and throbbing and melting until she was almost too weak to stand. His hand released her chin and dropped to her breast and she gave a plaintive little sigh of surrender and wound her arms around his neck, standing on tiptoe, and returning passion with passion.

And then quite suddenly he raised his head and put her firmly away from him, turning his face away so that she could not read the expression in his eyes.

"Odd's Life!" he said lightly. "Tis near incest, is it not? Making merry with thine uncle."

"You are not my uncle," whispered Alice.

"No. Only a phantom. I should not have punished you so, Alice. We will forget about it, shall we not? Tomorrow evening we shall start our search for a husband. It is well that these balls and parties go on all night or I should find difficulty in helping you."

Alice stared at him desperately. "Oh, Gervase," she cried. "I l . . ."

He quickly put a hand over her mouth to stifle the words.

"No," he said. And again, "No. You are tired my child. You must not take spirits such as myself seriously. We are nothing but air and fancy. See! I disappear. A new accomplishment."

He began to fade before her eyes.

"Please," begged Alice. "Please stay."

"Till tomorrow," came a faint mocking voice from somewhere near the ceiling.

Alice sat down and stared at the flickering flames of the fire. "I don't want a husband," she said fiercely into the silence of the room. "I want . . ."

But she did not know what she wanted apart from peace and security. Her strange, tumultuous feelings when he had kissed her she put down to a sort of supernatural power emanating from him.

Then she thought bleakly of the morrow which would bring a new companion. "She will be horrible, I just know it," Alice told the uncaring walls.

Miss Cassandra Fadden arrived at three o'clock the next afternoon. Alice entered the room, trying to hide her nervousness. She was determined to send this new companion packing. She did not trust the Duke's taste in companions.

At first she thought the drawing room was empty. Then someone gave a quiet little cough.

Miss Fadden was seated in a high-backed chair in the corner, her feet barely touching the floor. She was a gray, little woman—gray face, gray hair, gray shapeless dress, even her eyes were a washed-out gray. She wore a gray velvet turban which seemed too big for her small head. All her clothes, in fact, looked as if they had once belonged to a much bigger woman. Her shoes flopped at the end of her wrinkled gray stockings, her gloves hung from her elbows, and her false front of gray curls hung down on her forehead, leaving about an inch of skin between the curls and the hairline.

She looked harmless enough but Alice was determined to assert herself in case this gray ghost of a woman should turn out to be another Miss Snapper.

Alice patted her curls in the looking glass and then turned round and faced Miss Fadden. "Miss Fadden," she began and then said as sternly as she could, "*Alors, mademoiselle,* you are supposed to stand when I address you."

"I am standing," said Miss Fadden timorously. Alice blinked. Miss Fadden was indeed standing before her, having somehow moved from her chair. She was so small that it was like looking down at a child.

"I beg your pardon," said Alice. "My uncle suggested we might deal suitably together. Have you had experience as a companion before?"

"No, my lady," said Miss Fadden in such a quiet little voice that Alice had to lean forward to catch the words. "I am the daughter of a curate. Papa died two months ago and I was at my wits end as to what to do. I was sitting in the churchyard, crying, and suddenly this splendid gentleman appeared before me—quite like the Angel Gabriel, you know, except that I think his coat was made by Weston—no room for wings there—and he asked me why I was in such distress and I told him. He said his niece was in need of a lady-companion so here I am," she finished rather breathlessly.

Alice looked at her rather doubtfully. Miss Fadden looked quite old and frail. "Please sit down, Miss Fadden," said Alice in a gentle voice. "You would be expected to keep very late nights—very late," added Alice thinking of her ghost's restrictions. "Admittedly we would sleep a good part of the day, but I wonder whether you might not find the rigors of a round of balls and parties too exhausting."

"Oh no," pleaded Miss Fadden. "I should find it monstrous exciting. I have never been to a party in my life. Papa said such occasions were sinful. I'm glad he's dead," she added vaguely. "He will be so much more comfortable in Heaven, you know. He was not a good preacher, I am afraid. He always managed to make virtue sound like a threat."

Alice bent her head to hide a smile. Miss

Fadden was undoubtedly eccentric but she seemed gentle and kind.

"Miss Fadden," said Alice tentatively, "I had reason to dismiss my previous companion. To put it bluntly, she bullied me."

Miss Fadden waved her little gloved hand in protest so energetically that one of her overlarge gloves fell off and rolled on the floor. "Dear me, my lady!" she exclaimed. "I could not even bully the house cat."

Alice quickly made up her mind. "Then we shall deal extremely well together, I think. When would it be convenient for you to commence your duties?"

"Now," said Miss Fadden simply. "I am in modest lodgings in London and I have not paid the rent. They will be glad to see me go."

"Very well, Miss Fadden. I will send a footman for your belongings so as to spare you any embarrassment, and my man of business will settle your rent. Now, there is one thing I must make clear. My uncle, he has many affairs to attend to during the day so he is not free to escort us until the hours of darkness. We shall be setting out for our social occasions very late indeed. I do not wish this strange fact to be discussed in public."

"Oh, no!" breathed Miss Fadden. "My lips are sealed as with fish glue and they may torture and torment me but never a word will I breathe."

"Tiens!" exclaimed Alice. "It is not so serious as that."

"What is our first engagement, my lady?"

"My uncle has chosen the affairs to which we are to attend. He will inform us this evening of his plans. The first thing we are going to do, Miss Fadden, is to supply you with a wardrobe."

Miss Fadden clasped her hands together and stared at Alice as if she could not believe her ears. "Clothes. For me?" she said. "Oh, my lady, do I have to wear mourning? I have only these gray clothes since Papa deemed it seemly wear for a lady of my years. I had not enough money to buy black but I do so long to wear a *color* and no one in society knew Papa so they won't know I am supposed to be in mourning because, it is a sad fact my lady, but I do not *mourn*. He was such a *good* man, you see. And it is *so* hard to feel affection for people who are really good. Once he lost his sermon and kicked the cat and I felt a genuine rush of affection for him but he spoiled it all by praying over the cat and apologizing most humbly to it and for so long that the poor animal walked away in disgust."

"You can have all the colors you want," laughed Alice. "Come!" *Allez-vous en!"*

SIX

Late that evening, Miss Fadden sat in Alice's drawing room in a state of silent rapture. If she had not been so overwhelmed, so ecstatic over her shot silk ball gown and her new coiffure, she would have noticed something odd in her mistress's behavior.

Alice was nervously pacing up and down the room, dreading the Duke's arrival and longing for it at the same time. Had that kiss meant nothing to him? Of course it hadn't, she told herself severely. He was a philanderer and, by all accounts, had been one when he was alive. But would he notice her new ball gown of silver net worn over a silk slip of palest rose? Would he notice her black curls *à la Grecque*? Oh, horrid thought! Perhaps he would not come at all!

All at once she became aware that little Miss Fadden had arisen and was dropping a deep curtsy—so deep that she sank lower and lower onto the carpet.

"Uncle Gervase!" cried Alice, turning instinctively toward the fireplace. And there he was, in full evening dress, his jewels blazing in the candlelight. Did his eyes hold a new warmth as he looked at her?

Alice moved gracefully toward him, the silver gauze of her overdress floating out from her slim body. "I am so glad to see you," she said, trying to read the expression in his eyes.

He made as if to take her hand and then his blue eyes took on a mocking look. "My child," he said, "how charmingly you look. But I fear we should assist Miss Fadden."

Alice looked around and found that Miss Fadden had been unable to rise out of her curtsy and was lying on the carpet. With a sharp feeling of impatience at her companion's ill-timed gaucherie, Alice rushed forward and assisted that lady to her feet.

"Thank you, my lady," babbled Miss Fadden in great confusion. "What a bad beginning! What you must think of me. I shall try again . . ."

"No, don't!" cried Alice and the Duke in unison, but Miss Fadden was already sinking down. There was a sharp, embarrassing crack ing sound from her knees, but somehow with many grimaces, she managed to heave her small body upright. "There!" she cried triumphantly.

The Duke looked at her doubtfully and then said, "Miss Fadden. Pray excuse us. I wish to have a word in private with my niece."

Miss Fadden moved slowly to the door, her shoulders bent.

"Madam!" said the Duke, looking at her drooping figure impatiently. "Had my niece any doubts as to your suitability, I am sure she would not have engaged you. You are being sent from the room so that I may discuss some matters which do not concern you or anything about you."

Miss Fadden gave him a relieved smile and tiptoed out, closing the double doors behind her.

The Duke waited, his head cocked to one side, listening. At last he turned to Alice.

"What is it you wish to discuss?" she asked nervously.

"Why, your companion, of course. Miss Fadden. I fear she is not at all suitable."

"Oh, but she is so pleasant and so grateful!" cried Alice. "I simply could not turn her out-of-doors. She has never been a companion before, you see. I am sure she will learn very quickly. Oh, please let me keep her!"

"My child, if that is what you want, you may have it," replied the Duke, much amused. "Now, to our evening's engagement. We are to attend a ball at the Duke and Duchess of Haversham's."

Alice blenched. "What if they recognize me?" she cried. "I avoided them during the Season."

"We do not have to go to Wadham," he said. "The ball is to be held at their town house. I doubt if either of them ever set eyes on you before."

"But the servants," pleaded Alice. "They take some of the upper servants with them when they go to town. Mr. Bessant, for example . . ."

"He will hardly recognize the scullery maid, Alice, in the fascinating and beautiful young French Countess. Behave yourself! Odd's Life! I swear I can hear your knees knocking."

"I would rather not go," said Alice stubbornly.

"Then find a husband on your own," he snapped. "I shall go back to Wadham and continue my memoirs." His figure began to shimmer and fade before her eyes.

"No! Don't go!" capitulated Alice. "I will attend the ball."

"Then let us leave," he said quietly. "You have nothing to fear. Society is thin of social events in high summer. There is not much to choose from."

"But he will recognize *you!*" said Alice suddenly. "The present Duke, that is."

He shook his head. "I think not. I was not

in these modern clothes when I appeared to haunt him."

"The resemblance is nonetheless there. You look rather like him "

"He will not notice, my child. No man really knows what he looks like. Let us summon Miss Fadden and be off "

The Duke had seen to it that Alice had a splendid equipage in which to drive out. It was a yellow carriage with panels emblazoned with a well-executed shield and armorial bearings and drawn by two richly caparisoned horses. The Jehu on the box was dressed in a coat of many capes, a powdered wig and gloves *à la Henri Quatre*. Two spruce footmen in scarlet and silver livery with long canes in their hands completed the entourage

Little Miss Fadden sighed with pleasure and gazed out of the carriage windows with the wide-eyed interest of a child.

Alice sat silently at her side, the Duke facing her. She thought miserably that the whole business was a sad farce—being escorted to a ball by a ghost to meet a marriageable young man. Alice decided that she did not really like high society, despite the fact, that with the exception of Webb, she had so far avoided its major pitfalls. She had steered clear of the harpylike dowagers who were only too anxious to befriend a seemingly friendless and attractive girl as bait to lure men to the side of their bony and incoherent daughters. She had avoided the censure of the middle-aged dandies with their large appetites and weak digestions who hated so many and abused so many as they sat together in the bow window of White's Club in St. James's. She had received vouchers for Almack's during the Season—that center of snobbery—and had danced in those famous Assembly Rooms without once having fallen foul of the all-powerful patronesses.

She had no pushing mama to make her life a misery. She had seen so many debutantes, shy, demure, strait-laced and red-elbowed, forced to frisk and talk slang and wear wide-awakes and behave like the veriest Cyprians by their ambitious mothers.

The routs were the worst. There was often not even cards or dancing—only a tedious time crowding up a staircase to be received by the host and hostess, enduring the hard-eyed stares of the *haut ton*, and then fighting all the way back down again to endure a two-hour wait on the front steps for one's carriage to battle its way through the press.

Alice sighed. Her life seemed fated to be spent either among the highest in the land or the very lowest.

The carriage rattled to a halt in front of an imposing mansion facing Hyde Park. They had arrived.

"Now," whispered the Duke as he helped her to alight. "Head up! No one will take you for a scullery maid unless you behave like one."

Alice, head held high, swept in on the arm of the Duke. She was dimly aware of their being announced—"Monsieur Le Comte de Sous-Savaronne and La Comtesse de la Valle-Chenevix—" and of Miss Fadden, trotting behind, her mouth wide open as she stared about her at the flowers and hangings and jewels of the guests.

Then, facing her, were the Duke and Duchess of Haversham, just as she remembered them. Her heart seemed to miss a beat but they bade the Duke and Alice a chilly welcome with their customary indifference.

The ghost murmured something polite and then they were descending the stairs to the ballroom.

Alice forced herself to look at the guests. As far as she could see there was no sign of Lord Webb. Then she turned her attention to the servants. Not one familiar face.

She heaved a sigh of relief and decided to try to enjoy the evening.

"Will you dance with me?" Alice asked the Duke shyly.

"Of course not, you silly goose," he said. "You are here to dance with much younger men than I. Ah, here come some of your admirers. I will make myself scarce."

Alice half put out her hand to hold him back and then let it fall helplessly to her side. A fleeting look of lost bewilderment crossed her face and for a split second she looked very young and afraid.

That was when Mr. Bessant saw her. The Groom of the Chambers was looking down into the ballroom to observe the guests. He stiffened and grasped the rail of the banisters tightly, craning his head forward.

For one second he could have sworn that Alice, that scullery maid, had come back to haunt him. But then the young woman had turned to the first of her partners. She was laughing and flirting with her fan, the very picture of a fashionable young miss. He slowly relaxed his hold and shaking his head went off about his duties.

Alice promenaded after the first dance with Sir Peregrine Dunster, a merry young man with a mop of artistically windswept fair curls and laughing eyes. Alice listened to his chatter with only half an ear, her eyes scanning the moving throng for her Duke.

"I say," said Sir Peregrine plaintively, coming to a sudden halt and looking down at her, "you ain't listened to one word I've said. Now, I ask you. Am I such a bore?"

"N-no," said Alice, all pretty confusion. "I was looking for my uncle."

"Oh, that's all right," he said cheerfully. "I thought you was lovelorn. You know, sighing after some chap who ain't turned up."

"La! How could I search for another when I am with you, *monsieur?*" laughed Alice, waving her fan.

" 'Fore George, if your eyes ain't like pools

of violets. I used to write poetry, y'know. Wouldn't think it to look at me now."

He gave a mock grimace and Alice, who found herself liking him immensely, was about to make another flirtatious retort, when her face suddenly froze in dismay.

"What's the matter?" he asked, following her startled gaze.

Miss Fadden was sitting with the chaperones. Alice had been too preoccupied with her thoughts during the journey to the ball to notice that the companion had taken a small workbasket with her. Unconcerned at the haughty, startled gazes of the dowagers beside her, she had taken out a lumpy pair of half-finished gray socks and was proceeding to knit busily, a pair of very utilitarian steel needles flashing in the candlelight.

"Who's that tremendous little quiz?" asked Sir Peregrine.

"My companion," said Alice faintly. "I must speak to her. She should not . . ."

"Too late," grinned Sir Peregrine. "Here is your next partner."

Alice was swept off into a hectic English country dance and, for at least the next three quarters of an hour, had no time to worry about Miss Fadden.

Sir Peregrine turned to seek some refreshment since he was not engaged for the next dance and nearly bumped into a tall gentleman whom he recognized as Alice's uncle.

"I was watching you dance with my niece," said the Duke. "You make a pretty couple."

"Thank you sir," mumbled Sir Peregrine, although his mind raced. Was this French uncle trying to marry him off? And after one dance?

"Come! Let us find some refreshment," said the Duke imperiously and, without waiting to see whether Sir Peregrine was following him, he marched off to the supper room.

Lady Wilkes and Lady Bellamy, formidable dowagers both, bent their turbaned heads together. "Isn't it disgraceful?" hissed Lady Wilkes, the loose folds of flesh at her neck quite taut, for once, with excitement. "Knitting! In the middle of a ball, too!"

Lady Bellamy craned her tortoiselike head around her friend to stare at the offending knitter. The needles flashed hypnotically in the light as Miss Fadden's busy fingers bungled stitch after stich.

"She's not doing it properly," said Lady Bellamy. "She's about to turn the heel any moment and I don't think she *can*."

"Just ignore her, dear," replied Lady Wilkes. "'Tis unwise to encourage eccentrics."

Lady Bellamy bit her rouged underlip in distress. "But I hate to see such a mess. I declare I cannot bear it a minute longer. Do change places with me."

Startled, her friend complied.

"Now," said Lady Bellamy severely to Miss

Fadden. "That will not do at all, you know. You are making a sad botch of your stitches."

"I know," said Miss Fadden simply. "But I find it very soothing. But you are right. Perhaps since I *am* knitting, I should learn to do it well. Here!" she thrust the wool and needles into Lady Bellamy's hands. "Do show me."

Lady Bellamy cast an anguished look around. But the temptation was too much. "Very well," she said. "Now watch closely."

When Alice finally escaped from her partner, she headed straight for Miss Fadden, bent on reprimanding that lady.

But Miss Fadden by that time was surrounded by a whole court of elderly ladies. Turbans and feathered headdresses were bent over a piece of lumpy mangled knitting and the air rang with competitive advice. "It's not fair," remarked one elderly lady sourly, "why Miss Fadden should get away with bringing her work to the ballroom and I have to sit with my hands folded. I could show you all a thing or two. I have a good mind to despatch my John to fetch my workbasket."

Several startled glances were cast in her direction. "Why not?" asked Lady Bellamy, quite flushed with excitement. In no time at all, servants were being sent out into the night to bring workbaskets.

Alice's next partner claimed her and she wisely decided to leave Miss Fadden alone. It seemed as if the companion had found friends already.

Sir Peregrine meanwhile vas warming to the Duke. He had already drunk more claret than was good for him and it had loosened his tongue. "If you don't mind me saying so, sir," said Sir Peregrine, "you don't talk like a Frenchie, you don't even look like one. Damme, if you don't look a good bit like Haversham."

"Nonsense," said the Duke languidly. "I have lived in this country for the past twenty-four years. Left just after the Terror. I have practically forgot my native tongue."

"Oh well, then, stands to reason," said Sir Peregrine. "You said you left after the Terror. Weren't they after your head?"

"Of course," said the Duke simply. "I was . . . er . . . kept in hiding for some years. My parents did not escape. That is why I have the title," he added gently.

Sir Peregrine flushed. He felt as if he had just been guilty of some social gaffe. "Your niece is deuced pretty," he said to cover his confusion.

"She is very beautiful," corrected the Duke. "Alas! There are so many young men after her hand, I fear I do not know which one to choose."

"Indeed!" exclaimed Sir Peregrine, suddenly sobering. He felt quite piqued. He had thought this handsome uncle had singled him out as a suitor for his niece and was quite prepared to run for cover if that were the case, but now that it appeared there was, so to speak, already a long queue in front of him, he all at once remembered how attractive and charming he had found Alice.

"I have the honor of another dance with your niece, sir," he said hurriedly. "Perhaps I should go and find her before some other lucky man steals her from me."

"Yes, so many young men," went on the Duke as if he had not spoken. "She is a considerable heiress and I fear that is a great deal of the attraction . . ."

This was too much for Sir Peregrine. He had held an heiress in his arms and if he did not hurry, he might lose her. He got hurriedly to his feet and then remembered his manners and turned back to make his *adieux*. But of the uncle there was no sign. He had simply disappeared. He blinked and then headed rapidly for the door, nearly colliding with the Duke and Duchess of Haversham. He noticed that the usually glacial pose of the Duchess appeared to have cracked, but he was in too much of a hurry to wonder about it for very long.

"It's a disgrace!" the Duchess was saying. "And I cannot help feeling it is all your fault. First you philander with the guests at Wadham, and then you have turned my ball into a sort of sewing circle for gentlewomen."

"My dear," said the Duke of Haversham, very stiffly on his stiffs, "I have no control over the behavior of my guests once they are here, and for you to blame me for the antics of a parcel of elderly chaperones is beyond belief."

"I shall be a laughingstock," said the Duchess, clenching and unclenching her hands. "I have always been famous for my *ton*, for the elegance of my *soirées*. Look!"

The Duke sighed and looked again. Miss Fadden was surrounded on either side by a long row of chaperones, each with a work-basket. There was knitting and tatting and knotting and sewing and embroidery and tapestry and macrame. Voices were raised in gossip and hands were busy. Meanwhile on the floor and around the perimeter of the ballroom, their charges flirted outrageously, free from antique supervision.

Sir Peregrine was holding Alice in his arms as he led her through the steps of the waltz. He had fallen in love, he told himself. The fact that his tailor's bills and gambling debts could be settled by an advantageous marriage was pushed firmly to the back of his brain. He prided himself on being a romantic; he prided himself on being unmercenary. Now when a young Englishman plagued by duns sets himself to falling in love with an heiress, he makes a very good job of it and nearly achieves the real thing.

By the end of the waltz, Sir Peregrine's fine eyes were ablaze with love and Alice found her pulses beginning to beat a little harder.

The ghost watched them with an indulgent smile. He had removed himself from the supper room when young Peregrine's back was turned, as he did not want the present Duke to recognize his ancestor. He was conscious of someone staring at him. He turned around quickly but could see no one in particular. Then he looked up. Bessant, the Groom of the Chambers, was staring down at him from the musician's gallery. The Duke raised his quizzing glass and his eyebrows and fixed the Groom of the Chambers with an awful stare. Mr. Bessant flushed and retreated.

It was a mistake to come, thought the Duke. But the oaf, Bessant, cannot possibly recognize Alice as the missing scullery maid.

He watched Alice's happy smile and felt a faint twinge of pain somewhere in his chest. It was good that she could be happy with someone of her own age.

The Duke had investigated young Peregrine's background by talking to several of the guests. He came of good stock, was accounted wild and believed to be in debt. But the Duke had been all those things in his youth, and was, therefore, inclined to forgive wildness in one so young.

But so long as he stood and watched them— there! —Peregrine had definitely pressed Alice's hand—he experienced that strange pain. He decided to remove himself. Then he espied the glamorous blonde he had flirted with some months ago and headed happily in her direction.

Alice watched him over Peregrine's shoulder. For a moment, her wide eyes held a startled look of hurt, and then she firmly turned her attention back to Sir Peregrine and began to flirt for all she was worth.

Alice decided then and there to fall in love with Sir Peregrine. For deep down at the bottom of her hurt, a little flame of anger was beginning to burn. If the Duke wished to philander and kiss and fade away in that silly way, then the sooner she banished him from her thoughts, the better.

And so the young couple circulated gracefully around the floor, each hell-bent on falling in love with the other, the one for money and the other, for revenge.

Meanwhile, Mr. Bessant, that worthy servant, chewed his nails in a corner and thought furiously. He was sure he had been mistaken in the identity of Alice. But the appearance of the "ghost" at the same ball was too much for him. The more he thought back to the haunting of Wadham Hall, the more convinced he became that Alice had not committed suicide but had found an accomplice and both had tricked him. There had been a gaping hole found in the northeast corner of the wall in the grounds of Wadham, and rumor had it that someone had found the old Duchess's jewels and made off with them.

He decided at last to bide his time and to watch every movement the guilty couple made. He accordingly made his way back to the musicians' gallery and leaned over.

Of Alice's accomplice, there was no sign, and the girl he had believed to be Alice was pirouetting around the floor, looking so lovely and so aristocratic with a great collar of diamonds blazing on her neck, that Mr Bessant decided the light had tricked him

By the end of the ball, Alice had decided that she was definitely in love. She gracefully accepted an invitation to go to the play with Sir Peregrine the next evening and collected her companion and made her way out to her carriage.

She was looking forward to seeing her ghost when she got home—for she assumed that that was where he was, for she had not seen him for the past two hours—and telling him her joyous news.

But as she left the Haversham town house, a gray dawn was pearling the sky in the east and a thin mist was curling around the old trees in Hyde Park.

Alice gave a little sigh which sounded rather like a dry sob. She would need to wait and wait until darkness fell again in order to tell him how happy, how supremely happy, she was.

SEVEN

The Duke sat in Alice's pretty drawing room telling himself firmly that he felt very happy for her. He tried to fight down a feeling of pique. She might at least have waited for him instead of going off to the play with Sir Peregrine and Miss Fadden.

The room held two clocks, a sonorous grandfather and a chattering gilt French thing, and their noise appeared to grow louder and louder in the silence of the room.

At last he persuaded himself that it was his duty as "uncle" to attend the play and make sure that Alice was still as happy as she had seemed the night before. He had not hired himself a valet since a personal servant might have wondered at his master's odd appearances and disappearances, and so it was a good hour before he let himself quietly out of the house with his hair carefully dressed and his *chapeau bras* under his arm and his sword stick at his side.

The night was warm and balmy and he decided to walk. As he turned out of the square, he had an uneasy feeling that he was being followed. He turned quickly around and just out of the corner of his eye, he saw a shadow, slightly blacker than the other shadows, slink into a doorway.

The Duke walked on until he came to a point where the road was crossed by a narrow lane. He swerved suddenly into the lane and quickly practiced his latest trick, that of making himself invisible.

He waited.

At the crossing a tall figure came to a stop and turned his head slowly this way and that, his features momentarily lit by the flickering light of a parish lamp.

It was Mr. Bessant. The Duke drew in his breath sharply. He must warn Alice to be on her guard. Bessant must have recognized one or both of them at the ball. He cursed himself for having exposed her to danger.

Mr. Bessant hurried on. He could not understand where his quarry had disappeared to.

He had thought and thought since the ball and, in retrospect, it seemed to his agile brain too much of a coincidence that two people looking remarkably like Alice and her friend should have reappeared together.

He made his way along the street, head bent in thought. He felt a sudden brush of air past his cheek and a light mocking laugh sounded in his ear. He whirled this way and that, but, apart from himself the street was deserted.

The Duke made his way into the theater, avoiding the solicitations of the drabs who would do anything for a shilling's worth of rum. That at least had not changed since his day.

He purchased a ticket for the pit and stood at the entrance, his eyes raking along the row of boxes. At last he saw her, her face partly concealed by the red curtain. Miss Fadden was fast asleep beside her in one chair and Sir Peregrine was in the other.

Alice and Sir Peregrine were paying no attention to the stage but were gazing into each other's eyes. The Duke wished he had not come, but nonetheless, waited patiently until the end of the play which had only a few minutes to run. All at once, he decided to go back to Manchester Square and await Alice there. He would not spoil a promising courtship.

Feeling very virtuous, he made his way home. Again the clocks clattered in the gloom as he helped himself liberally from the brandy decanter. It was only as the night drew on that he realized he had had nothing to eat and the brandy was rising to his brain in an irritatingly mortal way.

One hour to dawn. Where on earth was she? He felt very injured. Were it not for him, then she would be scrubbing pots in the scullery and no doubt be big with child by that wretch Bessant. And this was all the thanks he got!

Then he heard the rumble of the carriage wheels on the cobbles outside and Alice's light laugh followed by a hearty masculine guffaw. She had brought Sir Peregrine home! This was the outside of enough. He strode into the hall and wrenched open the street door. Alice and Miss Fadden stood there, looking with startled expressions at his angry face.

"Where is he?" demanded the Duke.

"Who?" replied Alice, trying to move past him into the hall but finding her way barred.

"Don't be missish! Sir Peregrine."

"I don't *know*," said Alice pettishly. "We went on to the Hammond party with Sir Peregrine and we have just left there. I should think he is probably still there."

"Don't fool me," snarled the ghost. "I heard a distinctly masculine laugh."

Alice giggled. "Oh, that was Miss Fadden."

The ghost stared wrathfully at the companion who looked as faded and meek as ever.

Feeling obscurely that he was making himself ridiculous, the Duke stood aside to allow both ladies to enter. "Miss Fadden," he said, "leave me alone with my niece, I pray you."

Miss Fadden curtsied demurely and bade him a whispered, "Goodnight" while he stared suspiciously after her retreating figure. Surely such a quiet mouselike creature could not have had a laugh like that.

He walked into the drawing room, holding the doors open for Alice.

"Now, Alice," he said sternly, "I think you were remiss in not leaving me a note to say you would be so late. It is nearly dawn."

"It is indeed," yawned Alice in an indifferent way which made the ghost even angrier. "I danced and danced and danced."

"No more than twice with Sir Peregrine, I hope," he said. "We do not give rise to gossip."

"But we do hope to marry," said Alice, sitting up straight. "If it makes you feel better, we observed the conventions. Sir Peregrine," she added with a blush, "is all that is proper."

"I am overjoyed to hear it," said the ghost nastily. "But I do not think you should plunge into another engagement so soon. You are too precipitate."

"The whole point of the exercise," said Alice hotly, "is to find me a husband. Well, I have found someone kind and charming and . . . and . . .*young*. I think we should deal together extremely well."

"I hope he will ask me for my permission to pay his addresses," said the Duke.

"It is not necessary," said Alice sweetly. "You forget. You arranged for that decision to be mine alone."

"You must be guided by me . . ."

Alice was tired and her emotions were mixed and jumbled. He did not want her. Then why was he *nagging* her in this way?

"Oh, leave life to the living," she said petulantly.

There was a stunned silence while they stared at each other.

Somewhere, far in the distance, a cock crowed.

He began to shimmer and fade.

Alice wordlessly stretched out her arms to him, a look of intense pleading in her face.

Then he was gone.

She forced herself to think of Sir Peregrine, but somehow could not even visualize his features.

There was a timid scratching at the doors and Miss Fadden crept in, still in her opera gown. "I came to help you to bed, my lady, now that your uncle has gone."

"And how should you imagine my uncle has gone?" asked Alice sharply.

"Why, because 'tis dawn, my lady," said Miss Fadden. "Now, you are quite worn to the bone, I can see. Cassandra shall tuck you into bed, my lady, and bring you a posset."

Alice wanted to ask the companion what she had meant. Why did Miss Fadden not assume that Uncle Gervase had simply retired to bed? But, of course, that is what she had meant. She could not mean anything else.

It was some weeks later and the Duke was again closeted with his memoirs at Wadham. He had not returned to see Alice. He had washed his hands of the ungrateful minx. The living Duke and Duchess and the horrible Bessant were back in residence. Sometimes the ghost remembered that he had not warned Alice against Bessant's curiosity, but he shrugged it off. He would not admit to himself that Alice had hurt him deeply.

His window was open to the early autumn evening and sounds of music filtered up in the still air. The Duke and Duchess were entertaining again.

The ghost had just finished shaving his head. He had then donned his wig and his original silks and lace and felt much more cheerful than he had done in some time.

He eyed the sheets of quarto lying on the table and then found himself looking up into the mindless, vague eyes of his wife. He studied the portrait with some irritation. He had never liked Agnes, he decided, and he did not even want her painted image now.

With one impatient move, he pulled forward a chair, and standing on it, lifted the portrait down from the wall.

He drifted through the walls and corridors with it and at last left it lying outside the present Duke's bedroom door. He then decided to float invisibly about the grounds for some air. It was when he was drifting through the great hall just below the level of the ceiling that he looked down and saw a familiar face. Lord Harold Webb—and with him was his weedy friend Mr. Harry Russell. He gently descended to hear what they were saying.

It appeared that the friends were meeting again for the first time since the end of Webb's engagement to Alice and appeared quite overjoyed to see one another.

"I heard all about the Snapper business," Mr. Russell was saying. "Are you leg-shackled yet?"

"Not I," said Webb cheerfully. "The Snapper's gone where she can't cause any trouble."

"Where?" said Mr. Russell avidly.

"Madhouse," replied Webb laconically.

"How did you manage that?"

"*I* didn't. Father did, God bless 'im. Soon as he had calmed down, he saw the folly of it. Always been fond of me has the old man. Told him that yaller-haired uncle of Alice's had rigged it. So Pa gets boiling mad and says that Snapper must have gone along with the plot. So a little money here and a hand greased there, and the Snapper was carted off where she couldn't do any harm. Fortunately Pa don't ask me how Uncle Gervase could have managed it because I'm blessed if I know. But I tell you this, Harry, no one fools a Webb and gets away with it. Some way, someday, I'll fix that Frenchie pair."

The Duke saw the silent cadaverous figure of Bessant standing a little way away, listening intently to every word, and decided to put an end to the conversation. He slapped Webb hard across his handsome, pompous face.

"Gad's 'oonds!" gasped his lordship, falling back a pace. "How dare you, Harry!" And with that, he planted a flush hit right on the end of his friend's pointed nose. Mr. Russell retaliated by kicking Lord Webb in the shins. Webb seized a handful of Mr. Russell's hair and pulled hard. Mr. Russell scratched Webb's face.

The Duke drifted off happily into the grounds, leaving them to it.

In a rose arbor, the Duchess of Haversham was walking sedately on the arm of the Bishop of Devizes. With her free hand she was gesticulating to emphasize each boring point of her monologue.

The ghost eyed her with disfavor. She was all he detested in a woman—arrogant, frigid and unkind. Still invisible, he drifted up to the couple and seizing the Duchess's waving hand, thrust it neatly down the front of the bishop's knee breeches. The Duchess and the bishop came to an abrupt halt, the Duchess, her face a frozen mask of horror—too horrified to remove her hand. The bishop looked down in surprise and then a slow smile crossed his cherubic features. "Deary me!" he said. "One is never too old after all."

The ghost fled, chuckling, feeling he had performed enough mischief for one evening. As he reached the boundaries of the demesne he suddenly sobered. Was Alice in danger? His mind worked furiously. He had supplied her with an authentic background. No one would be able to touch her.

But the thought of Miss Snapper languishing in the madhouse chilled him. He must do something about that. But not now. He paced up and down until he had convinced himself that Alice was safe from any mischief.

He decided it was once more time to closet himself with his memoirs. If he did not overhear conversations, then he would not be disturbed. Alice had plenty of money and was supplied with every elegance and comfort. He had only himself to worry about. But his earlier exhilaration vanished. Alice's pretty, wistful face seemed to float constantly before his eyes.

"What a paradox," he muttered. "I am a ghost and *I* am being haunted!"

It was a pity he had resolved not to listen to any further conversations for he would have been alarmed at what took place later that evening.

The portrait had been found and was much exclaimed over. The present Duke marveled over its reappearance and decided to hang the portrait of Agnes, Eighth Duchess of Haversham, in the hall.

The house guests were asked to attend the small ceremony. Webb and Harry Russell, still smouldering at each other and looking very much the worse for wear, were present if not correct. Bessant was supervising the efforts of two footmen to lift the portrait into place.

Suddenly the Groom of the Chambers drew in his breath in a sharp hiss. His eyes were fastened on the necklace around the lady's neck in the portrait. In a flash he knew he had seen that necklace before. He had seen it round that so-called French Comtesse's neck.

He let out his breath in a long sigh. There had been no ghost—any more than there was a Comtesse or a Comte. It was that wretched scullery maid, no better than she should be, tricking the whole of the *ton* on the arm of her accomplice, and both of them financed by the late Duchess's jewels. His first impulse was to rush straight to his master and tell him the whole story. But the present Duke, now that he had seen no more of his ghostly ancestor, had become quite proud of the visitation, although he told no one the contents of the ghost's harangue. Also, there was still a little nagging doubt at the back of Mr. Bessant's mind.

He could, just could, be wrong. He needed help. But who?

Then he remembered the conversation between Webb and Mr. Russell. He would tell them—and make sure that Lord Harold Webb paid for the information.

So while the ghost immersed himself in his memoirs again in the secret room, Mr. Bessant arranged a meeting with Webb and Mr. Russell for two in the morning when he could be sure all the other guests were in bed. Harold Webb had admittedly stared at him very haughtily, but when he heard that Bessant could supply him with a sure means of revenging himself on that Frenchie pair, he became more cordial and agreed to the interview.

Webb was regretting his decision by two in the morning. His head felt fuzzy with the amount of wine he had drunk and he was a true aristocrat in that he had all those twinges in his bones—inherited from a long line of ancestors—that told him he was about to be asked for money.

He had ungraciously allowed Harry to come along with him since neither of them could really settle on who had hit whom first.

"Damme, if there ain't a creepy air about this place," commented Webb sourly as they made their way out into the grounds. They were to meet Mr. Bessant in a rotunda situated on a small knoll above the ornamental lake.

"It's your liver," said his friend sourly. "Take rhubarb pills. 'Fore you know it you'll be seeing folks going through walls again."

Webb stopped abruptly and turned majestically to stare down at his friend. "You ain't my friend any longer," he said grandly. "Go!"

"Shan't," said Mr. Russell indifferently. " 'Sides without me you ain't got any friends. Nobody else can stand you."

"They are all jealous," retorted Harold Webb, but nonetheless allowed his friend to follow behind.

Mr. Bessant was already there and waiting for them.

Webb soon found that his bones had not played him false.

"Before I begin," said Bessant, his cadaverous face oddly lit by a lantern placed on the floor of the rotunda, "I want to make one thing clear, my lord, I wish to be paid for this information."

"Depends what it is," said Webb, affecting boredom.

There was a long silence while Bessant chewed his nails and stared at the two men. A full moon rode out from behind a cloud, flooding the rotunda with added light. The rolling parkland of the Wadham estate lay silvered and spread out in front of them through the elegant pillars of the white marble rotunda. On one side loomed the vast bulk of Wadham Hall, its myriads of small windowpanes gleaming whitely in the bright moonlight.

"Well, it's like this," said Bessant, sitting down on a marble bench while Harold Webb frowned at the servant's forwardness in seating himself while his betters were still standing, "that there pair, the Comtesse de la Valle-Chenevix and her Uncle Gervase, they're imposters, see? And worse than that."

A crafty look marred Webb's handsome face. "How will I know if you are telling the truth?"

"My story will speak for itself."

"And how much for this believable story?"

"A monkey."

"What!" Webb's face grew quite flushed. "Five hundred pounds is more than a scoundrel like you could earn in his whole life."

"True," admitted Bessant. "But your lordship drops more than that at the tables at White's of a night."

This was indeed true, as Webb was a notoriously unlucky gambler.

"Give him the money," said Mr. Russell gleefully. "I always thought there was something shady about that precious pair." He leaned close to his friend's ear. "Think on't," he whispered. "You lost twice that to Brummell t'other night without so much as turning a hair."

Harold Webb brooded long and hard. At last he came to a decision.

"Very well," he said. "A monkey, it is. Speak!"

"Your note of hand, my lord," cringed Bessant, all mock obsequiousness.

"My word as a gentleman . . ."

"Your note," hissed Harry Russell, his eyes gleaming wetly in the moonlight.

"Oh, here it is." Webb sat down on one of the stone benches and scribbled out a note and handed it to the Groom of the Chambers. "Now . . ." he said impatiently.

And so Bessant began, talking in a low, hurried, urgent voice while his small audience listened amazed. Lord Webb at one point of the narrative found himself overcome with a strange superstitious dread. For some reason that picture of Alice and her accomplice fading through the wall seemed etched on his brain. But he was not normally an imaginative man and his fears were quickly banished as the story went on and his eyes began to gleam with excitement, especially when Bessant culminated his tale by producing an old, yellowed piece of parchment which he had torn out of a book in the library—a list and description of the late Duchess's jewels.

"We'll simply turn over this list to Bow Street," said Webb excitedly when Bessant had at last fallen silent, "and give them a report of our suspicions and let them do the rest.

"By George! I'll see that shameless couple hang on Tyburn tree yet!"

"If we took the matter into our own hands, my lord," said Bessant, "we could have our fun with the pair first—particularly the girl, if you take my meaning."

Harold Webb and Mr. Russell turned over

his words in their minds, savoring the implications. That high-and-mighty uncle brought to his knees, Alice begging and pleading for mercy, saying she would do anything ... anything ...

Webb ran his tongue over his suddenly dry lips. "When do we start?" he said.

Mr. Bessant straightened himself up. The servant had suddenly become the leader.

"We will bide our time," he said. "I cannot travel up to town. You gentlemen must report to me the jewels she wears."

"Don't be too long about it, laddie," said Mr. Russell rather sulkily. He thought Bessant was getting a bit above himself. "In the style she's living, the jewels won't last long!"

Now, the ghost, unused as he was to the inflationary prices of the Regency where a dozen fine India muslin handkerchiefs could cost as much as fifty guineas, did not expect the jewels to last forever. But he certainly did not realize how much it would cost Alice to run a house in town, a carriage, an army of servants and a constantly changing wardrobe, not to mention Miss Fadden who seemed to have no idea of the value of money at all, but encouraged her young mistress to buy the most expensive gewgaws on the market.

Then with the start of the Little Season, there was Alice's box at the Italian Opera to be rented, not to mention the vast bill for entertaining she was beginning to run up as she gave elegant little suppers, crowded routs and one ball to which the whole of the *ton* came to drink up her wines and eat her food.

And then there was the sad case of Sir Peregrine. So far he had not proposed marriage although the lovelight had not dimmed in his eyes. But it seemed that he was always about to be shot or have to flee the country because he could not meet his gambling debts and Alice had cheerfully, at first, lent him money.

She was unaccustomed still to the ways of the *ton* and did not realize that young men did not ask young ladies for money.

She also wondered why Sir Peregrine did not ask for her hand in marriage for that way he could get his hands on all the money she had. But Alice had been too openhanded and Sir Peregrine, finding that he could get what he wanted without having to marry to get it, continued to flirt expertly and escort her everywhere and take her money.

Alice had banished her ghost to the back of her mind. Perhaps if she had not been so determined to fall in love with Sir Peregrine, so determined to lead him to the altar and show a certain supernatural manifestation that she could manage very well on her own, she would have given Sir Peregrine his marching orders long ago.

Another thing forced her to keep close to Sir Peregrine's side. Everywhere that Alice went, Lord Webb and his unlovely friend,

Harry Russell, seemed to appear too. Their eyes were always fastened on her, studying every line of her dress and every single jewel she wore. Alice had noticed that Miss Snapper was conspicuous by her absence, but was too relieved at the fact to question further.

One chilly autumn day when the leaves in the London parks were already turning dusty brown and gold, Mr. Bower, Alice's business manager, called at Manchester Square.

He was a small, chubby little man with a perpetual air of sadness about him, making him look like a baby that has dropped its rattle.

His air on that day was sadder than ever. Madam La Comtesse, he explained, would need to sell more jewels to furnish him with the necessary funds to pay her staff and the rent of her house. Alice went gaily upstairs to the jewel box and threw back the lid. Could there be so few left? A cold fear clutched at her heart. She realized she had been handing jewel after jewel over to Mr. Bower, blithely thinking the box was bottomless. She realized she could not marry Sir Peregrine, even if she wanted to. For she somehow could not let her ghost know—should she ever see him again—that she had managed her affairs so badly. She would have to marry someone with money. In this decision, Alice was not being particularly hardhearted or mercenary. Love among the aristocracy was something you indulged in *after* you were married, but you certainly didn't let it interfere with anything so important as marriage settlements *before*.

She gathered up some of the remaining necklaces and brooches and went slowly downstairs to the drawing room. Miss Fadden and Mr. Bower were sitting with their heads together and started rather guiltily when she entered.

Mr. Bower stowed the jewels away in a wash leather bag and then took his leave, looking even more miserable than ever.

Alice sat down with a weary smile. She had become accustomed to sharing part of her worries with Miss Fadden. The companion was so quiet and noncommittal, it was rather like talking to oneself. And so, after some hesitation, Alice began to explain why she could no longer hope for a marriage with Sir Peregrine Dunster. So sympathetic a listener was Miss Cassandra Fadden that Alice found herself telling Miss Fadden for the first time about the amount of money she had lent Sir Peregrine. "Or I should say *gave*," she ended with another little sigh, "for I fear he is never going to have the means to pay me back."

To her relief, her companion did not look in the least shocked, merely contenting herself with leaning forward and pressing Alice's hand.

"So," Alice went on, "I shall have to disengage myself from being escorted everywhere by Sir Peregrine. It is a pity. He is such a merry young man. He made me forget . . ." Her voice trailed away for she could not possibly tell Miss Fadden or anyone, for that matter, of her ghost. "He is to call for me in an hour, Miss Fadden, to take me driving in the Park. Perhaps you would be so good as to tell him I have the headache."

"My dear, indeed I shall," said little Miss Fadden warmly. "In fact, you are looking rather *strained*. Perhaps it would be a good idea if you lay down in your bedchamber. You must not worry about Sir Peregrine. I shall explain matters *very* tactfully."

Alice smiled wearily and agreed to go and lie down. Poor meek Miss Fadden, thought Alice as she trailed up the stairs. She hoped her companion was able to cope with such a robust suitor.

Fair curls in artistic disarray, blue eyes twinkling with good humor, Sir Peregrine presented himself at the appointed hour. He was ushered into the drawing room to find its sole occupant, Miss Fadden, who was sitting knitting a pair of wool garters.

"Her ladyship getting ready?" asked Sir Peregrine cheerfully as he helped himself liberally from the decanter.

"Sit down, my young cully," ordered a harsh voice. Sir Peregrine turned round and gazed about the room in amazement but there was no one other than the little elderly companion who had put down her knitting and was regarding him with a fixed stare.

"Who? . . ." he began.

"I said, 'Sit down,' " grated Miss Fadden.

Sir Peregrine subsided into a chair and stared at her, wide-eyed.

The companion's normally vague face seemed to have grown harsh lines and to have coarsened somehow.

"Lookee here," went on Miss Fadden still in that frighteningly gruff voice. "You think that phiz of yours is your fortune and so far you ain't done too bad, have you my bucko?"

Sir Peregrine opened and shut his mouth like a landed pike and finally found his voice. "How *dare* you, madam!"

Miss Fadden gave an inelegant shrug. "Someone's got to. There's a name for the likes o' you that lives on females and I won't bother to dirty my gab with it. But listen! Harkee to me, Sir Peregrine Dunster. If you so much as set a foot in this house again, I shall tell the whole of the *ton* how you have been sponging on my sweet lady. You great bag o' starched wind. 'Course you ain't going to marry her when you can get what you want for the asking. But you've finally killed the golden goose. They'll be no more eggs for your breakfast, my darling."

"You stupid old frump. I'll . . ."

'You'll *what?*" Miss Fadden's grating contempt made him wince. She came and stood over him, her eyes no longer vague and myopic but flashing icy fire. "A pox on your threats, cully. I could have the Runners down on you and have you driven from the country."

Sir Peregrine arose to his feet, trying frantically to appear outraged and dignified and failing miserably.

"I shall pay back every penny," he said weakly.

A single word dropped from Miss Fadden's maidenly lips. The obscenity fell like a stone into the silent elegance of the drawing room.

"*You,*" sneered Miss Fadden, breaking the silence at last while Sir Peregrine mopped his brow. "How're you going to pay? Always that lucky win, eh? Well, find some other chicken to pluck."

"You, madam, are no lady," bleated Sir Peregrine, retreating toward the doorway.

Miss Fadden gave a mirthless laugh. "I ain't and that's a fact," she said. "Lucky for Alice, ain't it?"

She stared up at him malignantly and Sir Peregrine fell back before her stare. He swung on his heel and fled from the room, hearing Miss Fadden's sudden burst of horrid cackling laughter sounding in his ears.

Miss Fadden waited until she heard the street door slam and then she walked to the window and watched Sir Peregrine to make sure he was well and truly leaving the vicinity.

She was about to draw back from the window when she stiffened and leaned forward. Leaning against the railings of a house opposite were Webb and his friend, Mr. Russell.

They seemed to be comparing notes. Miss Fadden frowned. She knew somehow that that pair spelled trouble. She had already heard rumors of Miss Snapper's fate from her new friends who sat sewing and knitting with her at various parties.

After some time, she left the window and, crossing the room, rang the bell beside the fireplace.

When the butler answered the summons, Miss Fadden apologetically asked if she might have some tea if that was not too much trouble.

The butler inclined his head gravely in assent, privately thinking that Miss Fadden was a most tiresome mouse of a woman.

EIGHT

The ghost put down his pen with a weary sigh and rubbed at his cropped head. His added life due to the long winter nights had enabled him to finish his memoirs at last. The wind howled around the Hall as November gales swept in from the sea across the downs. The fire was crackling merrily, the shadows of the flames leaping over the paneled walls.

All at once, he thought of Alice with such an intense longing that he was quite shocked at himself. He shifted restlessly in his chair. Of course, he was lonely. That must be it. And now that he had finished all his writing he had nothing else to occupy his brain. But it would have been pleasant to have shared his supper with her, to have chatted over the fire as they once did. She was probably married to Sir Peregrine by now—or at least engaged. It was no use traveling to town to find out—it would only distress her.

The Duke would not admit to himself that it would distress *him* in the slightest. But there could be no harm in wandering through the house and finding a newspaper. She might be mentioned in the social columns. There might be a description of what she was wearing to some ball and who had escorted her.

He arose and, concentrating hard, drifted down through the floors until he came to the library. No newspapers. Then he realized that they had probably been taken off to the kitchens and, if he did not hurry, he would find they had already been crumpled up to light the bedroom fires.

At last he found a copy of the *Morning Post* neatly folded in the butler's pantry and carried it off to the seclusion of his room. He was about to spread it out on the table when he noticed his piles of manuscript. How strange to think he had been so immersed in his past life that he had almost forgotten the present. He picked it up and laid it carefully on the chair beside the fire in which Alice used to sit when she was emerging from the chrysalis of scullery maid.

Then he sat down at the table and spread out the newspaper at the social column. He stared incredulously at the forthcoming marriage announcements, wondering if his eyes were playing him tricks.

Alice, Comtess de la Valle-Chenevix was engaged again. But not to Sir Peregrine Dunster, but to a certain gentleman rejoicing in the name of Joshua Funk, Esquire, of Russell Square.

"Never heard of him," muttered the ghost. "And Russell Square! She's marrying a Cit!"

He chewed his lip and thought hard. Perhaps the members of the aristocracy had not been to her taste and she had been drawn to someone of a lower order. But what of Alice's background? For the first time, he began to seriously wonder about the identity of the girl's parents. That she could undoubtedly read and write had been unusual. He decided that instead of flying up to Russell Square, he would do what he could to trace Alice's background. It might even turn out to be respectable! And that would be a pleasant wedding present for the girl.

For night after night, he diligently scoured the countryside, searching in parish register after parish register. It was, at last, when he moved from the county of Sussex and extended his researches into the county of Kent that he at last found success.

He had been flying home after another fruitless night's search when the squat Norman tower of a church caught his eye. It was, he estimated on the marches of Kent and Sussex and one that he had missed in his earlier searches, for it was partly concealed from above from most directions by a strange knobbly hill.

He landed lightly in the churchyard and floated through the walls of the church. With tremendous excitement, Alice's name seemed to leap out at him. He was sure it was she. "Born 1793 . . ." Yes, that was the right date. "Daughter of Mary and Paul Lovelace of Hackett's Cottages, St. Dunstan's-in-the-Wold."

He could hardly go around knocking on doors for it was nearly dawn, so he had to content himself until the following night which fortunately for him fell as early as four-thirty in the afternoon.

He decided to call first at the local inn although it was little more than a hedge tavern.

A surly looking landlord was polishing tankards with a greasy cloth. Two local yokels sat hunched over a smouldering fire. The Duke ordered a pint of Lisbon and carried it over to the fire, drawing up a chair beside the two old men.

He gave a preliminary cough but the two men seemed sunk in some sort of bovine trance and did not look up. He noticed that their tankards were nearly empty and drew some silver from his pocket. "What is your pleasure gentlemen?" he asked.

The two ancient figures turned slowly in their chairs to face him and he waited patiently until his offer should sink into the primeval mud of their slow brains and possibly be lit by the marsh gas of a little intelligence.

"Urrr," said both in chorus at last, holding out their tankards.

"Very well," said the Duke, signaling the landlord with a jerk of his head and indicating that his newfound friends would have the same again.

When these brief courtesies were completed, the Duke tried again. "Do you know the whereabouts of a family called Lovelace?"

One of the old men began to weave slowly from side to side, an alarming mannerism which the Duke was to learn was the preliminary to speech.

"Urrr," he said, and spat in the fire. He turned and held out a dirty horny hand. "Name of Gadger," he said. There was a long silence and he began to weave again. " 'Er's Frimkin," he added, jerking his head at the other old man.

The fire crackled into sudden life. The landlord behind the counter began to whistle through his teeth in an irritating way.

Mr. Gadger began to weave again. "Un's dead," he said and spat in the fire again. Mr. Frimkin sat immobile on the other side of the Duke like a piece of carved mahogany.

"Dead!" said the Duke impatiently. "What? The whole family? There was a child . . . a girl called Alice."

"Urrr," said Mr. Gadger and relapsed into a maddening silence. The Duke felt in his pocket and found a guinea. He drew it out and held it in front of Mr. Gadger's rheumy eyes. "Think," he said softly.

Mr. Gadger held out his hand for the gold but the Duke held it away. "Information first," he insisted.

Now Mr. Gadger weaved so much that the Duke feared he was about to have a fit. Then the words came tumbling out from between his toothless gums.

"Lovelace, 'er was boatswain in the navy and cum here to retire as young man cos 'is chest was took poor and he coughed blood somethin' orful. Marries Mary Abbott, widow needlewoman she wur and they has a babby. Lovelace couldn't work on account o' 'is chest and so Mary stitched and took in washin'. Urrr. He dies arter babby is born and good riddance. Allus moanin' and whinin'. Mistress Lovelace works that 'ard. Stitchin' and washin' an' stitchin' and washin'. Liddle Alice 'elps 'er, see. Then Mistress Lovelace, 'er dies o' the fever and Alice becomes mazed i' the head. Wanders orf one day and h'aint bin 'eard of since. Urrr."

There was a long silence while Mr. Gadger stretched out a paw toward the gold which the Duke was tossing absentmindedly up and down in his hand.

"But, Alice," said the Duke suddenly. "The child could read and write."

"Urrr," said Gadger, weaving again like some ancient cobra, hypnotized by the gold. "Curate's missus taught child. Mistress Lovelace allus 'ad ideas above 'er station. Did curate's laundry for naught, see, so's babby could read." Again he reached out but the Duke had one last hope.

"This Mrs. Lovelace who was Mrs. Abbott before her marriage. What were her antecedents?"

"Urrr?"

"Who were *her* parents?"

"Bert and Jessie Apple. Them's dead too," said Gadger sulkily, feeling he was being asked to do a powerful amount of work for the gold.

"And what was Bert Apple? What did he work at?"

"Footman to Sir 'Enry Baggot down at Five Mile wen 'e was a lad. But 'e drank somethin' powerful after he married 'un and never worked again so Jessie Apple, *she* 'ad to labor to support 'im. Runs in families," added Mr. Gadger and then quite amazed at his own philosophy, he muttered it over and over again, "Runs in families," and almost forgot about the gold.

The Duke sighed heavily and arose to his feet after pressing the gold coin into the wrinkled, calloused hand. He had no shining respectable family to bring to his Alice as a wedding present, only a background of drudgery and death and pain and loss.

He had not stretched his mind out toward London for a long time, but as he flew over the sleeping buildings and fields on his way back to Wadham, the Duke felt that somewhere on the perimeter of his mind was a sad Alice, an Alice lost and lonely and in need of him. All that night long, he tried to banish her image from his mind. But just before dawn paled in the east, he decided wearily that it would do no harm to pay her one last visit.

Joshua Funk! What a name! What had taken the girl?

Mr. Joshua Funk eased his great girth in his easy chair and cast a baleful look at Miss Fadden who was sitting meekly in the corner of the drawing room, knitting as usual. His pretty fiancée had just entertained him to an excellent dinner and he felt that all that was needed to perfect the evening was that he should be left alone with Alice.

He had, he reflected sourly, never been alone with Alice. Even when he had proposed to her, Miss Fadden had been present. He could not drive himself and Miss Fadden had pointed out meekly that it was *not at all the thing* for Alice to be in a closed carriage, unchaperoned, with any man. He looked at the beautiful face of his fiancée and wondered for the first time what she thought about.

Alice had cultivated a careful, masklike

expression during the recent months behind which her brain worried about money and her heart mourned for her lost ghost.

She had not seen Sir Peregrine since the day Miss Fadden had sent him to the right-about. Spurred on by her dwindling finances she had diligently searched for a husband. Mr. Bower had invested her money wisely, and for some time it looked as if Alice might not have to get married at all but she had not yet learned the difficult art of economy and since she was scrupulously honest and thought everyone else must be so, she was cheated shamelessly by the tradesmen and even by her own servants.

Perhaps she might have kept out of parson's mousetrap had not Mr. Funk been so eminently suitable. He was a merchant, a widower, with a plump fatherly air about him. He had met Alice by chance on her last visit to the City to see Mr. Bower. Alice had sold her smart carriage in order to retrench a little and had been standing on the muddy pavement in the pouring rain, looking for a hack to convey her home. Mr. Funk, hearing the companion address her mistress as "my lady," sprang into action, offering his own carriage, the escort of his person, and finally insinuating himself into the drawing room in Manchester Square.

He made no bones about the fact that he was willing to exchange his great wealth for a wife's aristocratic background and once the marriage bargain was struck, that had seemed enough. But half-forgotten lecherous thoughts were beginning to burgeon anew in Mr. Funk's brain. His fiancée should at least allow him a squeeze or a kiss. But Alice was always polite and vague and formal—and always chaperoned.

She sat quietly opposite him, a fine diamond necklace blazing at her neck—some of the last of the late Duchess's diamonds.

Mr. Funk wondered whether to pluck up courage and simply order Miss Fadden to leave them. But there was something about the quiet chaperone which rather frightened him. Furthermore, his Cumberland corsets which had felt comfortable before dinner, were making their presence felt. The starched points of his collar were cutting little grooves into his chubby cheeks and the ribbons on his stockings had been tied too tightly and were causing shooting pains in his fat calves.

Passion fled before the more seductive thought of getting home and letting his man prize him free of all this constriction and misery.

Accordingly he at last rose to his feet, kissed Alice's hand with a rare burst of gallantry, heaved himself into his antiquated carriage and was borne off home to Bloomsbury. He was too sleepy to notice a smart little vis-à-vis following at a discreet distance.

When he entered his comfortable mansion in Russell Square and was just about to mount

the stairs to his bedchamber, he heard someone rapping vigorously at the knocker.

He half turned, his hand on the banister, to
watch his butler going to answer the summons. It was not necessary for him to issue
orders that he was not at home. His well-
trained staff anticipated his every wish.

He heard his butler's muted apology and
then a pompous voice raised in protest, "But I
have just seen him go in. Tell him Lord
Harold Webb wishes to have speech with
him. Jump to it, fellow."

Mr. Funk almost ran across the hall, so
great was the magic of a title. "My dear Lord
Harold Webb," he said, thrusting his butler
aside with one pudgy shoulder, "Come in!
Come in! I was about to retire. But no matter.
You shall take wine with me."

As Webb walked into the hall, two men
followed him. "My friends," said Webb, not
troubling to introduce the small weedy man
and the tall, cadaverous one who followed
him. But Mr. Funk was sure they were lords
as well and led the way into an overstuffed
sitting room, calling on his servants to bustle
about and bring refreshment for the guests.

"And to what do I owe the pleasure of this
visit?" asked Mr. Funk finally when he had
calmed down and seen to his guests' comfort
and had a breathing space to realize that
strangers, lords or not, did not arrive unex-
pectedly late at night at a gentleman's residence and demand admission.

He scratched at his nut-brown wig, carefully oiled with Rowlandson's macassar so that a passing glance would take it for real hair, and looked slightly more warily at Lord Harold.

"Mr. Bessant," said Webb, "is here to tell you an incredible story. You may need to brace yourself, sir, for even Mr. Russell—that's my friend here—found the intelligence a shock." Webb took a deep breath and pointed a finger straight at Mr. Funk's crumpled, babyish face.

"You, sir, are being most dreadfully deceived."

Mr. Funk's small pouting mouth fell open in surprise. "Go ahead, Mr. Bessant," said Webb, "and tell your story."

And so the fat merchant listened in increasing amazement and mounting wrath as the tale of Alice, the scullery maid unfolded, a servant so wanton as to take one of the late Duke's by-blows as a lover, steal the family jewels and set up in Town to trick the flower of the *ton*.

"I shall call the Runners!" gasped Mr. Funk when he could.

"Oh, the shame of it. I shall be the laughingstock of the City. I was so proud of marrying a Countess. I . . . ."

"I was engaged to the same woman myself," said Harold Webb in a low ringing voice. He was enjoying himself immensely. "But I do not think there is any need for this disgraceful matter to receive any publicity at all."

"You mean they are to go Scot-free?" howled Mr. Funk, his heart hammering against his ribs and his blood pressure mounting to the toposphere.

"No," said Mr. Bessant with a slow smile. "You leave it to us. We shall punish them and after that we shall drive them out of the country."

"It all seems very unorthodox," frowned Mr. Funk. "But why have you waited so long? You say you have known of this scandal for some time."

Lord Harold flushed slightly under Mr. Bessant's measured stare. So long as matters had been left with him and Mr. Russell, they had been content to play spies, following Alice around, taking a note of her jewels and sending the information off to Bessant at Wadham Hall.

It had taken Bessant's arrival in London on a week's leave to spur them into action.

"It does not matter," said Mr. Bessant. "The matter is being dealt with now. You will, of course, be obliged to help us."

"I?" said Mr. Funk, looking startled. "How can I help?" His brain worked feverishly. What did they plan to do with Alice? He himself thirsted for revenge, but not the kind of revenge he felt they had in mind. On the other hand, should he take Alice to court, he would have to endure the ridicule of all his friends.

"We have a plan," said Mr. Bessant. "You are to say nothing of this matter to Alice. You are to take her on a drive on Friday—in two days' time—to an address we shall give you.

"You are to say that you are taking her to see a relative of yours. Make sure that Miss Fadden does not accompany you."

"That will be extremely difficult," bleated Mr. Funk. "I was never able to get rid of that woman."

"You will get rid of Miss Fadden," repeated Mr. Bessant coldly. "A shrewd businessman like yourself should be able to arrange the matter."

"But I am not cut out for such abductions," pleaded Mr. Funk, looking down at his portly form.

"You have only to deliver her to an address we will give you and, once she is safely inside, you may take yourself off."

Mr. Funk hesitated. Webb looked all an aristocrat should be, but his friend, Mr. Russell, was unprepossessing, and Mr. Bessant frankly smelled of the servants' hall.

"A *gentleman* like yourself," said Webb suddenly, "will know that we are in the habit of meting out justice, just as our ancestors did, without resource to the courts."

Mr. Bessant nodded, thinking of a long line of rapists, womanizers and sadists who had made some of the aristocratic families what they were at present. But Mr. Funk thought of chivalry and knights and family crests and all those things he held most dear and gave a reluctant nod in unison with Mr. Bessant.

"Very well," said Harold Webb. "Friday it is. Now if you will furnish me with pen and parchment I will give you the direction and the time . . ."

The Duke had unfortunately delayed his visit to London until the following night or he might have discovered the plot against Alice. As it was, he arrived to find that Alice and Miss Fadden were attending the opera and made his way there.

He was pleased to note that Alice's engagement to a Cit had not excluded her from a place at the opera. For the opera was as exclusive as Almack's and money alone was not enough to gain you a seat there. There was a cult of deportment and snobbery which had begun at the opening of the century which was just beginning to reach its peak. Beau Brummell and his set ruled the clubs in St. James's Street and represented the male autocracy of fashion. The lady patronesses at Almack's Assembly Rooms in King Street represented the feminine. At the opera, they both united their forces to make sure that only the best, the most blue-blooded, the most elegant, had a claim to a seat. The opera, in fact, like Almack's, was a social function which completely outclassed the Court. A committee supervised the issue of every ticket and a man or a lady went to the opera, or did not, according to their social position. "Only sixteen officers of the Guards were found worthy of that honor."

The opera itself took second place to the company. One went, after all, to see and be seen.

It was more exciting to crowd "Fop's Alley" at the opera to see the peerless Mr. Brummell and the dandies—Mr. George Damer, Lord Foley, Mr. Henry Pierrepoint, Mr. Wellesley Pole, Mr. Charles Standish, Mr. Drummond and Mr. Lumley Skeffington—than to pay attention to the stage. The question of the evening was not, "Who is singing?" but "How well got up is Brummell?"

Alice was unsophisticated enough to enjoy the music but by now had enough town bronze to cleverly conceal the fact.

Music had charms to soothe the savage thoughts that normally plagued her—why *was* she getting married—would she see her ghost ever again?—why was Webb always about, always staring?

The opera was Mozart's *Magic Flute* and although it is doubtful if the composer would have recognized much of his work since it had been rather John Bullified, Alice could find no fault with it and sat in a happy trance through the first act.

But at the interval she had to give attention to her small court of admirers and her mind began to race as she smiled and chatted. That she could retire to a small cottage in the country and live out the rest of her days on the little money that came from the investments made for her by Mr. Bower never crossed her innocent mind. The Duke had gone to great lengths to launch her in society so that she might find herself a rich husband and she felt honor bound to fulfill his wishes.

Then over the curled and pomaded heads of her court, she saw the Duke and her heart missed a beat. His blue eyes were as mocking as ever and his dress as exquisite. His fair hair was very short but teased into some semblance of a Brutus crop and several of the ladies in the nearby boxes were staring at him in open admiration.

"Gervase," whispered Alice but he raised a finger to his lips and she gave a little nod and turned her attention back to her admirers.

The Duke studied her court through his quizzing glass.

Now which of these men could be the lucky Mr. Funk? All were in their twenties and showed all the hallmarks of fashion and high living. He recognized three of them from previous social engagements and after an effort of memory, recalled their names. The fourth, then, must be Mr. Funk. He was a tall, elegant young man with an imposing military mustache and sideburns. Not so bad, admitted the Duke reluctantly. Not bad at all.

Miss Fadden had watched the silent exchange between the Duke and Alice and she wondered about it. There was an atmosphere between the two, mused the old lady, more like that between lovers than between uncle and niece—but the French were an odd race! It was a pity he *was* her uncle, reflected Miss Fadden. The companion eyed the "uncle's" blazing jewels. A small fortune there. Surely Alice did not *have* to marry Mr. Funk. But Alice had said she had to and Alice should know.

Miss Fadden sometimes had her own ideas about this strange relative who only appeared after dark but even to herself, they seemed so wild, so *gothic,* that she shook her head and dismissed them from her mind.

And what would Uncle Gervase make of Alice's obese and vulgar fiancé? Alice's admirers had gone and the Duke had pulled up a chair close to Alice. Miss Fadden decided to listen to their conversation. There was some mystery about this pair and she was anxious to solve it. Miss Fadden felt that if she could find the answer to the mystery, then she would be able to prevent Alice, of whom she had grown very fond, from throwing herself away on a City merchant.

"I think Mr. Funk will do very well," whispered the Duke to Alice as the curtain rose.

"You have seen him?" exclaimed Alice.

"Was not he that tall military-looking young man who was here a moment ago?"

"No. That was Sir Angus Baxter."

"Then where is Mr. Funk?"

"At home, I believe," said Alice slowly

"You do not sound certain."

"I don't know. I think he is indisposed. He sent me a most odd note," said Alice crossly. "My dear sir, I have not seen you in this age and all you can do is ask me about Mr Funk!"

"Naturally," he said in a low voice. "He is surely the most important thing in your life."

Miss Fadden strained her ears. How English they both sounded. Alice's French accent became less and less daily. At least she had not reverted to the country burr of Alice, the scullery maid, but that was something even the sharp Miss Fadden did not know to listen for.

"We cannot talk here," Alice was saying.

"I shall see you later," replied the Duke. "I am going to pay a call on Mr. Funk."

"Don't," said Alice in loud alarm and was shushed from the neighboring boxes.

"Why not?" he mocked. "What is his direction?"

"I don't want to tell you."

"Then I shall find it," he said, rising. "Russell Square, I believe."

Miss Fadden was determined to have a word in private with Alice's uncle. Perhaps if he knew Alice was merely marrying for money, then he might help. As he left the box, she followed hard on his heels, murmuring an excuse to Alice. But no sooner was she in the long corridor that ran along the back of the boxes than she blinked in amazement. For there was no sign of the uncle. None whatsoever. He had completely disappeared into thin air.

Miss Fadden returned slowly to the box, thinking hard. This uncle became more mysterious by the minute.

The Duke soon found the address of Mr. Funk in Russell Square by questioning a butler who was out taking the night air. As soon as he was in range of the house, he made himself invisible and drifted quietly through the outer wall, finding himself in an over-furnished sitting room where a middle-aged portly gentleman was sitting in front of the fire, entertaining a stout middle-aged lady.

He thought himself in the presence of the fiancé's parents and was about to melt away to go in further search of Mr. Funk when the lady spoke. And what she said stopped him short in his ghostly tracks.

"And when is the wedding to be, Mr. Funk?"

"I don't know," replied that gentleman heavily. "I don't know if I shall get married, Mrs. Jeebles. Ah, me!" He sighed and mopped his forehead.

"Not get married, Mr. Funk?" exclaimed that lady. "And here's me, your oldest friend, telling everyone you was going to marry a real Countess! Has she changed her mind?"

"Not she," said Mr. Funk gloomily. "I have

recently been put in the way of certain information that makes it seem as if I might be making a mistake."

"But you can never cry off," said Mrs. Jeebles.

"It will be done for me. No . . ." Here Mr. Funk raised a fat hand to quell the lady's next question. "Forgive me, Mrs. Jeebles. I can say no more. I am to take the Countess driving on Friday and after that it will all be over."

After a short silence, the couple began to talk of mutual friends, and although the ghost listened long and hard, Mr. Funk did not refer to Alice again.

Seriously worried, he took himself off to Manchester Square. In the first place, he thought, Alice must have run mad to even consider leg-shackling herself to such an old barrel of wind. And secondly, what was it that Funk had found out about Alice? The truth? God forbid!

To Alice's surprise, when the Duke was ushered into the drawing room, Miss Fadden made her excuses, saying she must retire for the night. Miss Fadden had grown very fond of Alice and felt the girl might have a chance to unburden herself if she were left alone. "And if she does not," thought Miss Fadden grimly. "Then I will do the unburdening for her."

No sooner had she left than the Duke moved into the attack. The contrast of the young and beautiful Alice, glowing in an opera gown of jonquil satin trimmed lavishly with Mechlin lace, to the vision of the portly merchant he had just left, made his voice harsher than he had intended it to be.

"What on earth possessed you to tie yourself to that aged bag, Funk?" he demanded.

"I like him," said Alice, staring miserably at her white kid Kemble slippers. "He is kind . . . and . . . and fatherly."

"It sounds incestuous. Is he fatherly in thine bed, heh?"

"There is nothing like that, nor will there be."

"Fiddle! There will be nothing like that for the simple reason that the old turd does not wish to marry you."

"You lie!" said Alice passionately. "He *must.*"

The Duke's eyes narrowed. "Why must he? Are things gone as far as that? Are you with child?"

"No! No!" Alice raised her hands to her flaming face. "Why must you always think the worst?"

"Then what other reason is there?"

"I must get married and find a home," said Alice, not looking at him. "I am lonely."

"Then marry for love, damme!"

"Love?" said Alice dryly, raising her eyes to his. "What is love? It is frustrated lust, nothing more. What is marriage? Legalized lust."

"Do not be so cynical. It does not become you."

"I was quoting you," said Alice. "Do you not remember?"

There was a long silence. The Duke sat down and stared into space. He sat so still that his many jewels seemed to burn in the candlelight without a flicker.

"Perhaps I was wrong," he said at last.

"No," said Alice, suddenly desperate to see if she could hurt him as much as he had hurt her by his long absence. "Love does not exist. That much I have learned. I would settle instead for a comfortable home."

"And children," he said harshly. "Children fathered by Funk."

"Perhaps. If I am lucky," said Alice, staring at him, hard-eyed.

"Well for your information, lady, I called, invisible, on Funk to find him entertaining an elderly lady-friend, Mrs. Jeebles, and confiding that he had discovered something about you that makes a marriage with you impossible."

"No!"

"Oh, yes. And he is to take you driving on Friday and somehow during that drive the engagement will be terminated."

"It can't be true," said Alice desperately, while he watched her curiously.

"Why so shaken?" he demanded. "Do not tell me you have formed a *tendre* for that old parcel of stocks and shares?"

191

"Yes," said Alice wearily. "Yes."

The Duke rose to his feet wondering if he looked as murderous as he felt.

He did, and Alice cringed back in her chair. But she would endure anything rather than confess that she had squandered all the money he had so generously given her.

The Duke marched over and jerked her to her feet. "I am going to teach you a lesson, my minx," he said. "Look on it as part of your education."

He pulled her roughly into his arms and began to kiss her savagely. Alice fought as hard as she could against the wave of passion she knew would shortly engulf her. She beat at his shoulders with her fists until he roughly seized her hands and pinned them behind her back, holding her pressed against his chest and gazing down into those large, violet eyes.

The Duke bent his head again and this time he kissed her very delicately and gently, his lips moving softly against her own. Alice closed her eyes and knew for the first time what the poets meant when they talked about not being able to call your soul your own. Head, heart and body surrendered under his exploring mouth. And when, still holding her tightly and kissing her, he floated up with her through the ceiling, up to her bedroom and onto her bed, she surrendered to him completely; she was aware of no sense of shame, only a burning, aching need to give herself to him.

She held tightly onto his naked shoulders as the room seemed to turn and dissolve, until the only thing that existed in the reeling world was the warm, passionate body of the man, moving above her.

At last, all passion spent, he cradled her in his arms. "Odd's Fish," he muttered. "Oh, Alice. My only love what have I done to thee? I must go, dearest child. Canst not mate with a ghost. I will ruin thy life, sweeting. Thou need'st a real man, a man for the days as well as the nights."

"I love you," said Alice. "I cannot love anyone else."

"It will not do, sweeting," he said, putting her gently to one side. "I must leave thee."

He began to dress hurriedly while Alice watched him in blank misery.

As he turned from the looking glass after arranging his cravat, Alice stretched out her arms to him in mute appeal. Her black hair was tumbling about the ivory of her shoulders and her eyes were wide and dark in the moonlit room.

The ghost looked at her gravely and then a wicked smile lit up his handsome face.

"Stap me vitals!" he said cheerfully. "Why so serious? Damme, we will be mad together until the dawn takes me!"

He wrenched off his cravat and divested himself of the rest of his clothes at great speed. "Thou art the loveliest thing I have ever held in my arms, Alice. Come to me again. Come here my sweeting and we will further thine education. We still have the night and a few more hours of my life. Come to me, Alice!"

NINE

Miss Fadden was alarmed to say the least. She was a light sleeper and there had been sounds issuing from Alice's bedroom during the night hours which had disturbed her greatly. And now, here was Alice, all ready to go driving with her fiancé, face flushed, shadows under her dreamy eyes.

"What right have I to say anything?" thought Miss Fadden bleakly. "I think they might be imposters of some sort. I do not believe he is her uncle. But I am an imposter myself!"

For, truth to tell, Miss Fadden was not a curate's daughter, nor had she been mourning the death of her father when the Duke had come across her in the churchyard. She was in fact an elderly housemaid who had found she was to be dismissed without a penny after years of service to a merchant and his wife and large family.

She had stolen money and her mistress's clothes—hence the overlarge-sized gray wardrobe—and had taken a modest room in London. But she had only stolen a very little money and it had soon run out, leaving her in arrears with the rent; in order to escape detection, she had changed her accent from its coarse low London tones to a genteel simpering whisper which she felt matched her clothes.

She had come to care for her young mistress very much, at first simply out of pure gratitude and then because of Alice herself. "Had I been a *real* lady," thought Miss Cassandra Fadden dismally, "then I would be shocked. I would accuse her of being abed with her uncle. I would tell her of my suspicions; I would tell her I am sure that this Gervase is not her uncle and that he is not French. I am sure she is not French either. But, dearie me, she might dismiss me and then what would become of me?"

Miss Fadden's thoughts were interrupted by the arrival of Mr. Funk. And the appearance of that gentleman gave Miss Fadden something else to worry about. She had not damned Mr. Funk on account of his merchant class. He seemed a very grand gentleman to her. She had simply disapproved of him on the grounds that he was old enough to be Alice's grandfather.

But now she noticed there was something sneaking and furtive about the man. And, yes, she could swear he was afraid.

"Well, well, well, ladies," began Mr. Funk, rubbing his hands together and exuding an air of false jollity, alarming to behold. "Fine weather for a little drive, heh?"

"Yes," said Alice dreamily while Miss Fadden peered out of the window and up at the darkening sky.

"Er ..." went on Mr. Funk, clearing his throat, "since we are going to visit an old cousin of mine and a vastly respectable woman, I think we can dispense with Miss Fadden's services for the afternoon, my dear."

"Yes," said Alice in that same vague way. She found that nothing during this day was real. The only thing that seemed real to her was the memory of a warm pair of lips and the thought of the night to come.

But, *"No!"* said Miss Fadden at the same time and with unexpected force in one usually so meek. "It is not proper. I have told you before, sir, that until you are wed it is not fitting that my lady should be alone in a closed carriage with you."

"Oh, I say," said Mr. Funk nervously, looking at his fiancée for assistance. But Alice had a little smile playing about her mouth and her eyes were full of dreams.

Mr. Funk swung back to Miss Fadden and

encountered a look of such stabbing venom that his fat heart quailed. Let Webb and his friends cope with the woman. He most certainly was not going to.

"Very well, very well," he said, still with that false air of jollity which made Miss Fadden look at him narrowly. The ladies were both warmly dressed and bonneted and so they allowed Mr. Funk to lead them out to his carriage. Miss Fadden paused slightly, a strange feeling of foreboding at her heart. For this was not Mr. Funk's usual, old-fashioned but well-turned out coach, but a rather dirty box of a thing with peeling varnish on the panels and a villainous-looking coachman on the box. There were no footmen on the backstrap.

"We are to travel in *that!*" exclaimed Miss Fadden. "I trust we do not have far to go."

"My . . . my own carriage is being repaired," said Mr. Funk hurriedly. "I . . . I rented this for the occasion,"—which indeed he had. "We are only going a little way over to Surrey."

Miss Fadden's eyes tried to flash warning and dismay to Alice as she sat opposite her mistress in the evil-smelling interior of the coach, but Alice was still lost in rosy thoughts.

It was only after they rumbled over the Thames and were bowling past the mean factories and shanty houses of the Surreyside to take the road out into the country, that Alice at last appeared to come awake.

She suddenly focused her eyes on Mr. Funk

and said, "I believe you wish to terminate our engagement."

"Said nothing of the kind," spluttered Mr. Funk, desperate to arrive at their destination and get rid of the whole business for once and for all.

"Oh, yes you did," protested Alice. "You said to Mrs. Jeebles that you had found something out about me that made marriage impossible."

There was a shocked silence and Mr. Funk turned quite white. Alice turned quite pale herself as she all at once remembered she was not supposed to know anything about Mr. Funk's conversation with Mrs. Jeebles.

Mr. Funk said desperately, "I said no such thing. Dammit." He thought, Mrs. Jeebles must have been gossiping over half London. That's how Alice got to hear of it. But By George she gave me quite a turn for a moment.

Aloud, he went on, "I said something in a funning way to a Mrs. Jeebles. I can only gather she took me seriously and talked over half London. I am sorry."

Alice relaxed. "Yes," she said, "someone told me about it."

Then Alice realized that she really *did* want to be released from this engagement.

"Mr. Funk," she said gently, "before we meet your cousin, I feel I must tell you that I do not think we are suited. I wish to terminate our engagement."

Mr. Funk's first feeling was one of over-whelming fury. That this doxy, this scullery maid should sit calmly beside him, rejecting out of hand one of the richest men in the City of London. With a great effort he mastered himself and began to think pleasurably for the first time of the fate that awaited her.

"Very well," he said stiffly. "I do not wish to talk about it."

"But . . ." protested Alice.

"No! No more," said Mr. Funk, taking out a handkerchief and covering his face as though overcome with grief.

Alice looked sadly out of the carriage window where the snow was beginning to fall. She felt very guilty and miserable. Poor Mr. Funk! How she had led him on. Oh, how she longed to be back in Manchester Square. The light was fading already as the long winter's night crept across the barren fields. Alice looked down at the watch pinned on her dress. Four o'clock. She hoped the visit would not take long. And when on earth were they going to arrive?

As if in answer to her unspoken question, the coach swung off the road and began to rumble up the bumpy, weedy drive of some wilderness of an estate.

Mr. Funk removed his handkerchief and heaved an audible sigh of relief.

"My cousin's," he said cheerfully.

"What is her name?" asked Alice.

"Name. Oh! Emily Jeebles."

"Another Jeebles?" said Miss Fadden, her pale eyes boring into him.

"Er . . . yes . . . the Mrs. Jeebles we were talking about earlier is by way of being a relative. Lots of Jeebles among my relatives," said Mr. Funk transferring the handkerchief to his brow where a thin film of sweat had broken out.

Miss Fadden felt a cold hand clutch her heart. But the day was so dark, so ominous, that surely that was what was giving rise to her fears.

The carriage swung round and came to a stop in front of a bleak, square brick house with a pedimented entrance.

"Pray go inside and warm yourselves," said Mr. Funk after he had helped the ladies to alight. "I must see that this fellow stables the cattle properly."

"It is odd that you should care so much about rented horses," said Miss Fadden, her voice losing its usual meek tones and sounding loud and harsh in the still, cold air.

Driven to Thespian heights by sheer fear, Mr. Funk burst into a well-simulated rage. "You get above yourself, madam," he said sharply. "I did not make my fortune by ignoring the pennies. These horses, I would remind you, are rented and should I return them in poor condition then I shall have to pay for them." He turned impatiently to Alice. "My lady," he protested, "cannot you get this woman of yours to keep a still tongue in her head?"

But Alice had come out of her dreams and was beginning to share Miss Fadden's fears. "I do not think I want to meet your cousin," she said. "I think I would like to return . . . now."

Mr. Funk clutched at his head, knocking his wig to one side. "Gad's 'oonds!" he howled. "We are only staying for ten minutes."

"Oh, very well," sighed Alice.

At that moment, Miss Fadden espied the sharp features of Harry Russell peering from behind a dingy curtain on the ground-floor window to the right of the door. She recognized him as Webb's friend who always seemed to be spying on Alice.

Her fears crystallized and, seizing Alice's hand, she cried, "Run, my lady. 'Tis a trap!"

Mr. Funk leaped in front of them and Miss Fadden drove her fist straight into his nose and sent him reeling.

"Stop!" cried a loud compelling voice from the door and a shot was fired over both women's heads.

Shaking with fear, they turned about.

Mr. Bessant stood on the doorstep with a brace of horse pistols leveled at them.

"Better do as he says," whispered Miss Fadden urgently, "else he'll kill us." For in truth, cold murder peeped out of the Groom of the Chamber's deep-set eyes.

They walked slowly toward him and Alice

let out a cry of fear as he was joined by Mr. Harry Russell and Lord Harold Webb.

The coach, which was pulled over to one side of the building, wobbled slightly as the escaping Mr. Funk heaved his large bulk into it.

"Come in, Alice," sneered Webb, "and meet your trial, your judge, your jury and your conviction."

As they entered the house they heard the coach rumbling off down the drive. "Mr. Funk," said Alice, "he will tell everyone."

"Oh, no he won't," said Harry Russell practicing a villainous sneer and feeling quite like Kean. "He doesn't want the world and his wife to know that the great merchant, Mr. Funk, was thinking of tying himself up with a *scullery maid*."

"Yes," said Webb, more pompous than ever, "Not only a scullery maid but an imposter and a jewel thief."

"I am no thief!" cried Alice.

"You stole the old Duchess's jewels," said Bessant.

"I did not steal them. You must believe me. They were given to me by someone who had a right to them."

"Don't try that ghost story on me again," laughed Bessant. "That was no ghost. That was your lover pretending to be the Eighth Duke of Haversham." Miss Fadden's dazed mind seemed to grasp onto one thing. Ghost! Of course!

Alice looked about her wildly. The house was empty and deserted. No furniture. No servants. Miles from anywhere. But she had so much to live for. Her life, her love.

She made a wild dash for the door but found her way blocked by the grinning Bessant who had nipped quickly in her path. She threw herself upon him, raking his face with her nails while Miss Fadden lashed out wildly at the other two. Bessant swore and, raising the horse pistol, brought it crashing down on Alice's head so that she fell like a stone.

"Pity," he muttered, looking down at the unconscious girl. "Now I won't be able to get the whereabouts of that so-called uncle out of her till she comes to."

Webb and Harry Russell had succeeded in subduing the ranting, raving and cursing Miss Fadden, but not before she had kicked Harry Russell in both shins and blacked Lord Harold's eyes.

"What language!" exclaimed Webb, quite shocked. "Sounds like a sailor, don't she? Better gag her as well."

"Now what do we do?" asked Harry Russell gloomily. "Can't have any fun till she wakes up."

To tell the truth both Mr. Russell and Webb had felt rather squeamish at the idea of helping Bessant carry out his revenge but now that the thing had actually been set in motion in this house so far from anywhere, it had aroused nasty age-old instincts and they were only too anxious to begin.

Mr. Bessant smiled obsequiously, reverting to the servant as was his habit when he was not actually taking any action. "I took the liberty of bringing a cold supper and some very good claret, gentlemen. You will find it in the next room."

"Splendid chap," said Webb. "What about Alice? What if the girl recovers her wits while we are dining?"

"Tie her up too," said Bessant, touching Alice's still body with the toe of his boot. "She can wait."

The Eighth Duke of Haversham smiled dreamily at his reflection in the looking glass. He had dressed in the clothes he had worn when he first saw Alice. It was a romantic gesture and he felt he had never been romantic before.

He was bejeweled and scented and patched and powdered. He found it rather awkward to walk about in his red high-heeled shoes for he had become accustomed to wearing Hessian boots most of the time.

It was just at that point that some awful, harsh, grating voice seemed to shriek inside his head. "Help, sir!" it cried. "Your niece is in danger. Help! We are somewhere in Surrey. Outside Richmond, I think. Oh, help! They'll murder us."

He put his hands to his ears but the voice cried on and on.

Paralyzed with fear, he stood motionless, listening to the terrified voice ringing inside his head.

And then all at once he was off and out of the Hall out under the black sky and flying over the silent fields, flying faster than he had ever done before, pulled always by the harsh crying of that frightened voice.

Alice let out a faint moan and tried to sit up. She found she could not, for her arms and legs were tied. The bare room was lit by a single tallow candle and in its flickering light, as she twisted over on her side, she could see the bound and gagged figure of her companion. Miss Fadden's eyes were staring at Alice in mute appeal, trying to convey some desperately important message and all at once Alice thought she understood what the companion was trying to say.

The room swayed and whirled as Alice was overcome by a sick feeling of dizziness, but she fought against it and concentrated with the whole of her mind on the Duke. What if he heard her but did not come? What if he did not love her? What if the grave had reclaimed him? And what if he had only been philandering? But after a few moments, the effort of concentration was too much for her. Her head hurt so much that she let out a cry and immediately afterward, realized her mistake.

The sound of voices in the next room abruptly ceased and then there was the sound of approaching footsteps.

The door opened and her three kidnappers walked in.

"Now," said Mr. Bessant smiling down into Alice's wide and terrified eyes, "we shall have some fun with you. Tell us first where your so-called uncle is, and perhaps we will not be quite so hard on you."

"I don't know," whispered Alice. "I wish to God that I did."

"Then if you must do things the hard way . . ." began Bessant.

"Oh, no need for that, dear chap," said a light, mocking voice. "Do them the easy way and look this way. I am here!"

Alice gulped with relief. Miss Fadden closed her eyes in gratitude that her prayers had been answered.

The three men looked wildly about the room, but apart from themselves and the two women, it was empty.

"The wind," said Mr. Bessant. "We're hearing things."

"Look outside the door," urged Harry Russell.

Bessant who had shut the door behind them when they had entered the room, turned the doorknob and then looked over his shoulder at the other two. "It's locked," he said in a flat voice.

"Of course it's locked, my angels," said that mocking voice again. "Now we can be cozy."

The fireplace had been piled high with dry kindling. Now it miraculously burst into flame. The three men backed closer together.

"That's better," went on the voice. "Now you will release these ladies immediately."

Mr. Russell made a move but the more courageous Mr. Bessant held him back. "I'll see you in hell first," said Mr. Bessant.

"Then I shall take you there," laughed that maddening voice and then to their horror a figure began to glimmer and glow in front of the fire.

White and shaking, the three men clutched onto each other.

The figure shimmered and changed in the flickering firelight and all at once seemed to solidify.

Magnificent in his gold brocade coat, knee breeches and powdered wig, the Eighth Duke of Haversham made his bow.

"Gervase!" sobbed Alice. "I love you."

"My sweeting," said the ghost severely. "This is neither the time nor the place to unbosom yourself. La! But I must play the gentleman. You force me to blush in front of these low types and tell you that I love thee with all my heart, my Alice."

He walked over to her as he spoke and drawing his sword, quickly cut her bonds.

"Now Mr. Bessant," he said, turning on that gentleman who was making moaning sounds of fear. "I believe you wish to go to hell. Come!"

He caught hold of the terrified Mr. Bessant and started to drag him toward the fire.

"Look out!" cried Alice.

Mr. Bessant had raised a horse pistol and was pointing it straight at the Duke.

There was a deafening report and then Mr. Bessant began to scream with terror. For all at once there was no Duke. Nothing but the empty air and the wild screaming following the report, and the harsh sobbing of Mr. Russell.

"I . . . I . . . hem . . ." said Webb and collapsed in a dead faint.

"I am tired of this," said the Duke's mocking voice as he suddenly materialized again.

"Come, Alice. Take my hand. Miss Fadden, hold tightly to my other hand."

Miss Fadden went to him in a daze, wondering why she did not feel in the least frightened. Would his hand be as cold as the grave? But it was reassuringly warm and human and she clutched it tightly.

Alice held onto the other, white and shaken from the blow on her head but feeling happier than she had ever felt in her life before.

He had said he loved her.

Webb came out of his swoon with a groan. In front of his staring eyes, the Duke flanked on either side by Alice and Miss Fadden, was backing slowly toward the outer wall. Harry Russell was sitting on the floor with his face buried in his hands and so was the only one of the villainous three who did not see the last of the ghost.

But to Mr. Bessant and Webb it was the horror of horrors. The three melted right through the wall, stood for a moment *outside* the window, looking in, and then slowly began to rise up.

There was a thud and a crash.

Webb had fainted again.

It was midnight. The Duke, Alice and Miss Fadden sat in the drawing room in Manchester Square, silent at last. Alice had recovered quickly from the blow on her head although she was still looking white and ill. Miss Fadden's busy hands were idle at last. The Duke was wondering what to do.

He felt sure that none of those villains would dare to start babbling about ghosts in case they ended in Bedlam, but on the other hand he did not want to leave Alice unprotected again.

"I have a confession to make," said little Miss Fadden suddenly breaking the silence. "I am not what I seem to be, Your Grace."

The Duke surveyed her with a marked lack of interest. "None of us is," he said dryly.

"But you don't understand," said Miss Fadden. "I am not a lady. I was nothing more than a housemaid who was being turned out into the street because I was too old. I . . . I . . . stole a little money from my employers and ... and ... some of my mistress's clothes."

"Then you had better stay with us," said the Duke rudely interrupting this painful confession. "I am a ghost, Alice is a scullery maid and we will all have to discuss our future." His voice softened as he saw the companion's distress. "Do not worry, Miss Fadden, I shall take care of you as well."

"I have a confession to make as well," said Alice in a low voice.

"I am sure it is nothing so terrible my love," said the Duke, "that it cannot wait until you are rested."

"I must tell you now," said Alice wretchedly. "I have spent nearly all the money from the jewels. Mr. Bower advised me long ago to invest the money in stocks and shares but I did not think it mattered until too late. Now there is a certain return, but very little. And ... and ... there is worse."

"My sweeting," said the Duke, "was that why you wanted to marry the terrible Mr. Funk?"

Alice nodded. "And ... and ... I lent money to Sir Peregrine. Such a lot. And he never paid it back."

"You were silly," said the Duke, "but understandably so. My child, I have all my own jewels. I was a great peacock in my day and had so many to leave to my heir that a sentimental aunt insisted that quite a number of them were buried with me. It's a miracle the resurrectionists did not try to dig me up. I shall deal with Sir Peregrine in my own way. This is all trivia. My worry, is, what is our future? You are young and beautiful, Alice. You do not wish to be tied for life to this old phantom."

Alice stood up and went over and knelt beside his chair, taking his hands in hers and looking up at him. Miss Fadden scampered from the room with surprising speed.

"I love you," said Alice simply. "There must be some way we can spend our life together. I cannot live with anyone else but you, my very dear ghost."

He held her hands tightly and at last the old mocking smile lit up his mouth.

"Then so be it, my Alice," he said, drawing her up onto his knee. "We shall celebrate the nights together. We will remove ourselves to some place where our strange behavior will not occasion comment. Now get thee to bed, my child. There are things I must do before we leave London . . ."

Late the following afternoon, just as the light began to fade, Mr. Funk sat in front of the fire at his club in Lombard Street in the City and stared into the flames.

It was the *silence* that was unnerving, he decided. No word from Lord Harold Webb. He had sent a footman to the gentleman's residence only to receive the reply that Webb had gone out of town.

He still smarted over the idea that Alice was only a scullery maid. Somewhere in his fat heart, he viciously hoped they gave her a hard time. In retrospect he thought he could remember all sorts of common qualities about the girl. But the late nights he had spent worrying over the silence from the three conspirators plus the heat from the fire and the effects of a heavy lunch, began to take its toll. His head nodded and in no time at all, he was asleep. His last thought before he dropped off was a certain gratitude to Webb for having saved him from ridicule.

So fast asleep was he that he did not feel the light flick of a paintbrush over his face.

He awoke with a start some two hours later and glanced at the clock in alarm. The Lord Mayor's banquet! If he did not hurry, he would be late.

It was only a step to the Mansion House. He would walk. The club room was empty. In his hurry, he did not even feel the nimble fingers pinning a notice on his back.

It was the talk of the City coffeehouses for ever afterward . . . the night that Mr. Funk walked straight into the Lord Mayor's banquet, his face painted a bright, bright blue and with a placard on his back bearing the legend, "I am in a Blue Funk."

How they roared with laughter and clasped their sides and fell about, those City men. Mr. Funk had long been detested for his pomposity.

So, thanks to the ghost, the merchant did not escape ridicule after all.

Sir Peregrine Dunster had his hands on a fortune . . . literally. He had his hands tightly on the waist of Miss Hetty Withers who had just accepted his hand in marriage. She was a considerable heiress, newly in town, and for once Sir Peregrine had moved briskly into the attack before anyone else had had the chance.

Miss Withers was an ironmaster's daughter and the ironmaster, Mr. Adam Withers, was bedazzled with the idea of his daughter becoming a lady and had allowed Sir Peregrine to pay his addresses without inquiring into his character.

"Oh, Sir Peregrine," sighed Miss Withers, "you make me the happiest of girls."

He smiled adoringly into her myopic eyes, ignoring her bad teeth and rabbity mouth. He did not want to kiss her. Delay it. "Why don't you call your papa in and we'll tell him the good news," he laughed.

But her parents burst into the room as if they had been leaning on the outside of the door, which in fact they had.

As a beaming Sir Peregrine turned to face them, he suddenly felt himself go cold all over and then to his horror his mouth opened, or rather it felt as if it had been prized open, and a voice, not his own, came out. It said, "I hope you know I'm only marrying your Friday-faced chit for her money."

The Withers gasped in unison.

Sir Peregrine clamped a hand to his mouth and to his horror a ghostly hand seemed to drag it away.

Too terrified to do anything other than stand and stare, Sir Peregrine heard that horrible voice issuing from between his now white lips.

"I thought an old fool like you would be taken in by my title," it sneered. "Odd's Fish! Just look at your stupid faces. Do you really think I would marry this rabbit-faced quiz for her *looks?*"

Mr. Withers rang the bell so furiously that in no time at all three of his footmen had erupted into the room.

"But . . . but . . . but . . ." said Sir Peregrine.

"Throw him out," screamed Mr. Withers, pointing a shaking finger at the hapless Sir Peregrine. "Throw him in the kennel where he belongs!"

And that is exactly what they did.

The Duke took his leave of Sir Peregrine's now filthy body and floated up over the London streets. He had just one more job to do.

The Duke alighted some time later outside the gothic gates of a madhouse outside London and rang the bell.

At last he was admitted and demanded to see the principal.

"I am the Duke of Haversham," said the ghost grandly, neglecting to say which one. "I believe you have a Miss Snapper confined here. I take leave to tell you she is sane."

The principal Mr. Jorry bowed before the magnificent figure of the Duke but nonetheless hesitated. "Miss Snapper was confined here, Your Grace," he said, "by the express command of the Earl of Markhampton. She screamed for weeks that she was sane but to tell the truth she seemed madder than anyone else here."

"I assure you she is sane," said the Duke firmly. "Are you going to dither there and maunder on about what a mere *Earl* said?"

This was argument enough for Mr. Jorry.

And that is how a bewildered and tearfully grateful Miss Snapper—fortunately still sane—found herself released by no less than the Duke of Haversham and furnished with references and a tidy sum of money to start her in life again.

The Duke cut short her paean of gratitude by remarking acidly, "If you ever bully anyone again, Miss Snapper, may the same fate befall you," and it was only long afterward that Miss Snapper wondered over his marked resemblance to Alice's Uncle Gervase and how he had come to know that she had been in the habit of bullying anyone at all.

The present Duke of Haversham bit his nails and looked sideways at the chilly face of his wife. "My dear," he said tentatively, "do you believe in ghosts?"

"No I do not!" snapped the Duchess. "I believe in *facts*. I know you are a philanderer, sir, and that is a fact."

"Indeed," sneered the Duke. "I, of course, have not yet gone so far as to assault a bishop but no doubt I shall sink to your low standards one day."

The angry couple glared at each other with hate. Their rage lasted many days and was only assuaged for a short time when they mutually agreed to fire the Groom of the Chambers who had become so meek and frightened that he was of no use at all.

"... Ms. Dean," he said reproachfully, "do you believe in ghosts?"

"No, I do not," I replied. ... the Quakers...? believe in men. I know you are whatever ...? say, and that is a fact."

"Indeed, ..." ...? "I of course have felt ... ? so far as to haughtily ... ? but no sooner, I still think to your ... we have there any day."

"The three people ... ? says, they who held their ... the ghosts had ... four seats of him, a short time when they ... sort of ... into the ... room at the Chamber, who had had a scene, and gone ... frightened thither was to be thrust out."

EPILOGUE

Miss Fadden leaned back contentedly in her cane chair and watched a large red sun sinking slowly down into the blue of the Mediterranean.

Below her, the terraced gardens fell away in ordered beauty to a small curve of white sand. She stretched like an old tabby cat and picked up her knitting. Just a few more rows and it would be time to wake her mistress.

It was paradise, she reflected, this crumbling castle on the Sicilian coast. No one came to call, the few servants were paid well to be discreet, and the happiness of her master and mistress permeated every room.

Then she heard Alice's light step and leaped guiltily to her feet. "The sun is not yet down, Your Grace," she said. "I thought you would sleep longer."

"He will soon be here," said Alice, Eighth Duchess of Haversham, leaning her elbows on the warm balustrade and staring dreamily out over the sea.

Miss Fadden watched her with a doting smile, remembering their flight from the bitter cold of London, the uncertainty as to where to stay, the travel, the inns, the flying over strange towns and villages, and then finally the homecoming to this remote spot.

The sun disappeared into the water with a flash of green and one by one the first stars came out. Miss Fadden knew that the Duke would make his appearance below in the garden and come walking up the steps as he did every night so as not to alarm the servants by appearing suddenly, say, at the dinner table.

"What if he does not come?" whispered Alice suddenly. "What if he does not come?"

"He will come as he has done every night since we arrived here," said Miss Fadden in a brisk voice.

"Every night is a miracle," said Alice.

And all at once he was there, at the foot of the steps, smiling up at her and she looked down at him with all her heart in her eyes, holding out her arms as if to welcome him back from a long journey.

Miss Fadden tactfully removed herself to supervise the preparations for dinner. She was always relieved to see them together again but she was a sentimental soul and the sight of their happiness always made her cry.

The strange disappearance of the pretty French Comtesse caused some speculation in London circles, but by the beginning of the Season, everyone had found more interesting things to talk about.

Lord Harold Webb felt quite himself again. It had been a truly terrible winter. He had started and trembled at every sound. He had shunned the company of Harry Russell, feeling sure that it was that gentleman's black soul which had brought the ghost upon him.

Once more he was fêted and petted by matchmaking mamas. Once more debutantes fluttered their fans and eyelashes at him.

He leaned against a pillar under the musicians' gallery at Almack's and drew a slow breath of relief. The world had once again righted itself, the sun shone during the day and the flambeaux and candles of the rich blazed to banish the night.

Neil Gow's fiddlers were sawing away at a new waltz tune but for the moment he was content to watch the gaily shifting throng and know again that he was one of the handsomest and most sought-after men at the Assembly.

One of his former flirts, now Mrs. Annabelle Delacey, paused to speak to him as she walked around on her husband's arm.

She was a vivacious redhead with a rather piercing voice.

"Why, tis Harold Webb!" she cried. "My dear man, you look a ghost of your former self. A very *ghost!* What on earth have you been up to?"

"There are no such things as ghosts!" screamed Webb suddenly, drowning out the noise of the fiddles above his head, drowning out the chatter of voices of the throng.

Mrs. Delacey drew back a pace in alarm.

But Webb went on shouting and shouting, "There are no such things as ghosts!" until they led him away.

"Really," said Mrs. Delacey, much agitated, to her husband, "What was all that about? How strange to become so exercised. After all, we all know there aren't any ghosts."

Do we ? . . .

The Legends of the Old West
Live On in Fawcett Westerns

☐ VENGEANCE TRAIL   04663 $1.95
    by Dean Owen

☐ PAYOFF AT PAWNEE   04671 $1.95
    by L.P. Holmes

☐ BUCHANAN'S BIG FIGHT   14406 $1.95
    by Jonas Ward

☐ THE UNTAMED BREED   14387 $2.75
    by Gordon D. Shirreffs

☐ LITTLE BIG MAN   23854 $2.95
    by Thomas Berger

☐ HONDO   14255 $2.25
    by Louis L'Amour

☐ SWEENY'S HONOR   24330 $1.95
    by Brian Garfield

☐ RETURN TO ARAPAHOE   04590 $1.75
    by Charles N. Heckelmann

☐ CROSSFIRE TRAIL   14276 $2.25
    by Louis L'Amour

Buy them at your local bookstore or use this handy coupon for ordering.

COLUMBIA BOOK SERVICE
32275 Mally Road, P.O. Box FB, Madison Heights, MI 48071

Please send me the books I have checked above. Orders for less than 5 books must include 75¢ for the first book and 25¢ for each additional book to cover postage and handling. Orders for 5 books or more postage is FREE. Send check or money order only. Allow 3-4 weeks for delivery.

Cost $_____   Name_____

Sales tax*_____   Address_____

Postage _____   City_____

Total $_____   State_____ Zip_____

*The government requires us to collect sales tax in all states except AK, DE, MT, NH and OR.

Prices and availability subject to change without notice.

8197

CLASSIC BESTSELLERS
from FAWCETT BOOKS